DOUBLE DISASTER

SHADOWS OVER ELISTA, BOOK 3

CLARA WILS

Gryphon's Gate Publishing

Double Disaster

Copyright © 2022 Clara Wils

Gryphon's Gate Publishing
550 King St. N.
PO Box 42088 Conestoga
Waterloo, ON
N2L 6K5

Print ISBN: 978-1-990587-14-6

CHAPTER 1

DAWN

My sword never connected with the silvery fur of the White Wolf.

A roar, unlike anything I'd ever heard before, shattered the northern night and all of us — humans and wolves alike — froze. Then, the wolves turned and sprinted away into the darkness.

I felt it through my spirit-gift, the presence of something large and dangerous approaching, and it was unlike anything I'd felt before. With my enhanced hearing I caught the heavy, padded footfalls of several creatures approaching slowly. I looked, peering into the darkness.

"Spirits," I breathed at the sight of what could only be a Karhukora. I finally understood all of the conflicting reports I'd heard of them: related to wolves, but like a bear, large but fast. The beast was over eight feet at the shoulders, with fur like the wolves I'd just seen: silvery-white. The head was massive, perhaps slightly too large for the giant body, and was some strange cross between a bear and a wolf. Their fangs were even larger than the wolves we'd just been threatened by, and they had the same cold-blue eyes reflecting the light of our fire. Then, there were the claws on each oversized paw: easily over half a foot long as they tapped and tore at the ground with every slow step.

And behind this beast, others strode out of the darkness.

Thankfully, all of the giant beasts had riders. Each Karhukora held up to three burly men or women, in furs of the same silvery-white. Even more of these fearsome northerners walked beside their mounted companions.

"It's them!" Iko shouted. "The Njorvasoturi. They found us!"

"Iko, is that you?" The voice came from one of the mounted men, a rumbling base. "I never thought to see you again, young one." The large man easily threw himself down off his oversized mount and came forward. The man's face was mostly covered by a bushy beard and long wiry, tangled hair, both heavy with streaks of grey.

"Grandfather?" Iko said, peering at the man.

The man laughed. "I'm not that old, young one. No, your isoisa passed last winter. I'm your uncle, Mauno." With several long-striding steps, he was in front of Iko and embracing the young man. "When your father fled south, I thought I'd never see you again. How is my brother?"

Iko's face darkened. "He's dead, Uncle." Iko peered

into the man's face for a long time, a slightly forlorn look in his eyes. "I... I'm sorry Uncle, but I don't remember you."

Mauno grimaced, or so I assumed from the movement of his beard. He nodded. "I was not around a lot when you were a boy. Your father and I... didn't agree on much. He wanted to settle, I wanted to hunt." Mauno shook his head. "I'm sorry to hear of his passing. May the Hallowed Lights guide him to the arms of our ancestors."

"The Thraians killed him."

"Is that a disease?" Mauno asked, confused.

I almost laughed at that, though there was little mirth in me at the moment. We had found those we had come to find. Now we needed to get back south again and help Lyran.

And Roo... Though I knew that was near to impossible. Yet, I still felt the terror and pain radiating from her, far to the south.

She is strong, she'll survive this, Amya said, stoic. Yet, I was little comforted.

"No," I said finally speaking up. "The Thraians are a people, and in some ways, they are like a disease, but far worse."

When Mauno looked at me, he flinched, stunned. His gaze found Pan, then returned to me. "Are you spirits?" he asked, voice soft.

I blinked at that. It took me a moment to understand. Here I was, a tiny woman — when compared to these people — with an intense spirit which he could probably feel, but not explain. Also, my eyes glowed. Pan was similar.

"Close enough," I said. I was part Fey after all. And I did have *a spirit* within me.

I'm more than just 'a spirit,' Amya said, indignant.

You are, indeed. Apologies.

"I came with Iko and Eiva to find you. We need your help in the south. The Thraians have invaded and captured many of the northern villages of people who were once of your clans." Or so I understood things. "We need your help to drive the Thraians back south again. Iko's friends and village are in trouble, as are those I love. Will you help us?"

Mauno looked to Iko. "Who is this woman?"

"A miracle," Eiva said softly beside Iko. "We had forgotten our warrior ways. Our village was taken so easily. Many were taken as slaves and conscripts of the Thraian army. The rest of us... we hid." She seemed ashamed of this, but in truth there probably hadn't been much they could have done at the time. "But then this amazing woman arrived and reminded us of who we were, who the Njorvan could be once again. We plan to fight back, but we need your help; please."

Iko nodded along to this.

Mauno looked from Iko to Eiva. "Has this woman claimed you as her kihlattu?" Mauno asked. "She is fierce and would make a good wife."

Eiva blushed.

Iko stammered: "A-a-ah, n-no uncle, not... yet?" Iko finished with a slightly sheepish look at Eiva.

Mauno laughed. "I can see you southerners have gone soft indeed." He looked at the four of us.

The other Njorvasoturi had gathered around us. There were perhaps thirty or forty of them with a dozen Karhukora.

Mauno looked over to a woman with fine lines on her face and hair which was mostly white. I caught the significant look which passed between them, then the woman gave a single nod.

"The Hralsed clan will help you," he said with a similar single nod.

Interesting. So that woman had the true power here.

"Are there other clans?" I asked quickly. "How many?"

Mauno's bushy brows shot up. "It's been some time since our last Kokus. But there were seven clans who attended. I believe there are others as well. But we range all over the north. Some clans might never meet during a warrior's lifetime."

Interesting. "What would it take the gather them, all the clans, for war?"

Mauno straightened, to his full height, which was a match for Lyran, if not taller, though not as tall as Rhino. "War?" he said gravely. "Whose war?"

And that was the sticking point. The empire would probably never come this far north. These people were safe here, and I was asking them to fight in a war which would otherwise never affect them. This was someone else's war, not theirs. But... Spirits we needed their help. Trained and hardened hunters and warriors charging into battle on their massive beasts. That would be... a significant addition to our rebellion indeed. But how could I say that?

Just say it, Amya said, reminding me of my own power with words. *Just be yourself, be honest, and let your spirit shine. For these people, I believe the persuasiveness of your argument will not come from your words, but from you yourself.*

I nodded. *Thank you.*

I sighed, but met Mauno's gaze evenly... No... I turned and spoke to the woman Mauno had spoken to. "You are the leader of this clan, yes?"

She smiled, one brow raised, and nodded.

"There is a war in the south. The Empire of Thraan has already conquered many lands and they threaten many more, including my homeland. So, I will freely admit, I am not entirely impartial in my plea. And to be honest, the empire will probably never come this far north. Your people will be safe if you remain here. This is not your fight." The woman's face was hard, like stone, as she listened.

"But... if you remain up here and do nothing, the rest of the world will eventually fall under the shadow of this dark empire. There have been none who could stand against it, my nation has an army of fifty thousand men, and they will fall to this empire, most likely."

The woman finally spoke, her voice as hard and cold

as the barren tundra around us. "And if your thousands cannot defeat them, how shall our few clans? If we are safe here, why should be die in vain in the south?"

"If you scoured all of the north. How many might you summon?" I asked. "If there are fifty clans like yours, strong and stout, well trained, with your magnificent Karhukora, that would be a fearsome force indeed. That addition to the many others I hope to bring to our cause may just make the difference. And!" I felt a surge of energy. "If we can defeat this one army, I know we can start to push the empire back. We can save people, free them from slavery and conscription. You are all free up here in the North, would you deny that freedom to those to the south? Or... would you hear the name of the Njor-vasoturi shouted as saviors and liberators." I caught a flicker of emotion on that stony face, but I wasn't sure exactly what it was. "I know you live hard lives here, and the beasts you hunt are fierce indeed, but if you truly seek to test your mettle, to see how devastating the Njorvaso-turi can be, then join me, fight the Thraian Empire, free the south and you will have songs to sing of great victory for many, many generations to come."

"Well said," Pan breathed, beside me. He reached over to stroke my back through the many layers of our clothes and coats. His amethyst eyes glowed, filled with awe and love.

The Njorvasoturi woman looked at me for a long time before saying. "You possess great spirit little one. What is your name?"

"I'm Dawn."

A grim smile spread on the woman's face. "Dawn. The rising sun. Yes, an apt name. I am Astraed of the Hralsed Clan." She regarded me for a long moment. "The rising sun has great significance for our people. Our winters are long and dark, an endless night. And in the spring the sun rises again, and it is a day of great celebration when it does." She looked around at her clan. "Our life is harsh. We have fewer and fewer younglings who survive to adulthood. We are mostly old men and women, and I have seen the same among the other clans." She looked out into the darkness for a long moment. "We live in these lands because we have always lived in these lands, or so we believe. But there are ancient tales of our peoples in the lush lands of the south. We hunted and roamed free on green plains. Yet... as more and more towns rose up, our lands diminished. We were driven north to find other lands to roam, since settlement was not our way. We claim these lands... because no one else will." She sighed. "And that is a weak reason to exist." She looked to me again. "Perhaps it is time we returned to the south, but if we do... will there be lands there for us? Will we be welcome there?"

That was an interesting question. "Yes," I said without hesitation.

"You can make this promise?" Astraed asked, one brow raised. "One woman?"

I smiled. "I can." Because I'm radical, because I'll make it happen. "Because once you have liberated lands and we have destroyed the empire there will be lands aplenty to occupy. I am a leader among my people and one of those I travel with is a leader among his." And hopefully Lyran would be running the empire after all of this. If he was going to give back lands, then I was certain he could find someplace for the Njorvasoturi. "We will find a place for the Njorvasoturi to hunt and live free, where the winters are not dark."

Astraed studied me for a long moment.

"You are spirit-touched, Dawn," Astraed said. "And though I do not know how we might find such lands again, I believe you. I do not know how one woman shall make it happen, but perhaps you can. So yes, we shall come south with you. We shall gather all the clans and fight for you."

"And you won't be alone. We will gather other armies to our side, other allies. Oh and, did I mention... we have a dragon?"

That got a few surprised looks. They were hooked now.

CHAPTER 2

SWIFT

In my form as a swift, I had watched the battle and seen Lyran fall.

I swooped low over where the horn-bearer hid at the side of the battle and chirped as loud as I could. As I darted away, I caught the man putting the horn to his lips and heard the creaking roar of the Grymhallar. Now our forces would retreat. And not a moment too soon. Most of the enemy camp was awake and fighting back. We hadn't done nearly as much damage as we'd hoped. My only thought now was to save as many of these northerners as I could.

And Lyran.

I darted down and transformed back mid-flight to land a double-legged kick on one of the Thraians crowded around the dragon lord.

Landing with my twin swords out, I laid about me

savagely. I'd been trained in combat since I was nine and these past few months, with Lyran's tutelage, I'd grown in my ability.

I was aided by a few of the men and women in Lyran's troop as well, as they retreated. We cleared the area around Lyran, but...

"Spirits!" I breathed. The man was dead, he had to be. There was so much blood, coming from multiple gushing wounds, including a half-caved-in face.

Check his neck, Isoa insisted. *He's tougher than any normal man, perhaps...* but the Lumani didn't sound convinced Lyran was alive.

I bent and checked the man's pulse. I was surprised to feel the weak beat. "Spirits," I whispered again.

Give me strength, I told Isoa and then slipped my arms under the large man to heft him up. Lumani could lend a bit of strength to their hosts, converting their own spiritual energy into physical power. I felt that surge of vitality even as I staggered under the weight of this heavy man and his armor. Isoa's strength steadied me, and I was able to awkwardly run for the forest. Lyran's troop was all around me, keeping the Thraians away as we retreated into the darkness of the woods.

Still, I couldn't stop to tend to Lyran. The Thraians might scour these woods. There was a rally point for our forces, I had to make it that far at least.

"Is he...?" Reira, a northern woman who'd been Lyran's second in his troop was running next to me.

"He's alive, he's a tough one. We need to get to the meeting point. Do you have any healers in your village?"

"No true healers, a few herbalists, but... none here with us. Any who survived the Thraians are back in the cave now."

"Pits!" I cursed. "Then strip him of his armor and bandage him as best you can once we're at the rally point."

"What will you do?" she asked.

I had a sneaking suspicion I was going to have to: "Stop a raging dragon."

With Isoa's strength, I remained strong and ran fast through the forest to the rally point. There I laid Lyran down and Reira went to work on him with the help of others.

I veered and launched up through the trees into the sky. Swifts flew day and night and my night sight as a bird was good enough to see the massive shadow sweeping through the skies toward me... Eophon.

Isoa... ah... any thoughts on how to stop them?

I felt Isoa's hesitation. They were a new Lumani. I was only their second host. Still, as an immortal spirit they'd been around for a while. *I can feel their spirit. Perhaps... let me try to reach out? From what Lyran has said, they can only communicate with humans telepathically. But...*

Yeah, I know.

Neither of us knew whether Eophon could only communicate with Lyran — the human to whom they were bonded — or every human.

Let's try, I said, coming to soar alongside the massive, and very intimidating, form of the dragon.

Eophon! Please hear me! I felt more than heard Isoa's words, which were not meant for me.

Hush little human, my bonded is hurt, I must destroy those who did this!

On the one hand, I was very glad that had worked and we could communicate. On the other hand... *how in The Pits are we going to convince a dragon to keep to the plan?* I asked Isoa.

Let me try something, they said. Then to Eophon: *Please, mighty Eophon. I know you are hurting, but Lyran is still alive and may still yet survive this. You know just how tough he is. And as long as he lives, then should we not keep to the plan? If you attack now, that may only make things worse for everyone here... including Lyran.*

They were persuasive words. I hoped they worked.

We flew in silence in the height of the night's sky before Eophon finally growled, a frustrated sound and spun, turning away from their path. *I will do this on one condition. Bring Lyran to me, I may be able to help him.*

Seems reasonable, I said to Isoa.

Indeed, they said.

We followed Eophon, who landed at the edge of the forest. There they crouched, impatient and clearly agitated. Their long tail whipped about, the bone-blades at the tip flared out, thrashing trees like wheat, a terrifying sight. I darted into the woods back to the rally-point and transformed back. Several people were helping to bandage Lyran, who still seemed alive, but...

"Spirits," I breathed again. Seeing him naked, and the full extent of his wounds, I didn't know how he could be alive.

Lend me more strength, I said to Isoa, and they did.

"Wait," I called to those bandaging him. "I need to take him to his dragon. They aren't far from here. Come with me and bring bandages and supplies with you."

They all heard the word dragon and froze, stopping their ministrations. I went to Lyran and lifted the limp form. He was lighter without his armor on, but not by much. It seemed most of his considerable weight was the solid muscle on the man.

"Anything I can do?" Fria came to me just as I made to leave."

I tried to think quickly and only one thing came to me. "Take a dozen of the best archers among those who remain. Run as fast as you can and cover the road on the other side of that enemy camp. Hopefully, they haven't already sent runners south with news of the attack. If you see any, make sure they don't get past you. If the entire force is heading back south, great, don't engage them. Only if they're sending messages. Got it?"

She nodded and ran off.

Then I ran for everything I was worth. I didn't want Lyran to die. He had become a friend to me and... to Dawn...

If he died, Dawn might never forgive me. I couldn't

live with that. Dawn and Roo were... my everything, my world, my life. And I couldn't have anyone they loved perishing if I could help it.

Also, I didn't want to piss off a dragon any more than I already had.

When I reached Eophon, I laid Lyran before the giant creature. *Please do what you can for him.*

By The Sacred Flame! I heard the dragon's curse. Eophon bowed his long neck and touched Lyran softly with his long snout. The man glowed for just a moment, then the night was dark again. I heard the heavy breath, felt the hot air, as Eophon gave a sigh. *He is too far gone. I cannot restore him. I have done what I can to slow his decline, but that is all I can do now.* That head swung up to me. *Tell me again, little human, why I cannot burn those who did this?*

I experienced true, abiding fear in that moment, as a massive dragon glared at me, only a few feet away. Their eyes radiated power, smoke snarling up from that massive maw.

I had no real answer. I repeated Isoa's words. *As long as he lives, please keep to the plan.* And it was a good thing I was speaking in my mind; I don't think my voice would have worked with how terrified I was.

Eophon gave a blast of heated air which washed over me. I yelped in a very unmanly fashion.

I will wait, for now. But if those who did this come near this village we were to protect, I will destroy them. They weren't happy.

I couldn't really argue that point.

Agreed.

And that was that. I just hoped if Eophon did engage the enemy it would be to wipe them out. I didn't want to think of what would happen if word of a dragon reached the south.

CHAPTER 3

CEPH

Prince Demir had designed his enclosures well. Rhino, Falcon, and I were stuck in our avatar forms, forced into jails too small for us to transform and escape. Falcon was squished into a cage, feathers poking out from the bars. It couldn't have been comfortable, and I could hear the intermittent screeches he let out to punctuate his pain. Rhino was in a tiny cage, with a bit of room to walk around in his beetle form, but he was just as trapped as the rest of us. My prison was a box. Demir must have known about the 'slippery' nature of octopuses, how they can fit through small holes. So, the only hole available to me was the tiny keyhole used to unlock it.

I assumed it had been Lady Nazla who'd betrayed us and told the prince of our avatar forms, but she hadn't known about our other abilities. Meaning, as much as I couldn't slip out of this box as an octopus, I could still use

my spirit-gift of physiological manipulation to force some
of me out through the keyhole. I had done so, forming an
eye on the end of that tiny stalk to look around. That was
how I'd become aware of our predicament.

There were two guards in the room, sitting and chat-
ting and occasionally glancing over at us. Our cages were
on a table, out in the open, in the middle of the room. I
retracted my stalk and considered my options. I could use
my spirit gift to get out of my cage, but that was it.
Without a key, I'd not be able to help the others out of
their cages. Which meant I'd probably have to take those
two guards on my own.

Knowing that, and knowing stealth would be my
greatest ally, I began my slow and ponderous escape. I
sent a few, extremely thin, tendrils of myself up and out
of the box, to pool on the table, on the far side of my
box from the guards. I slowly reformed there. It took
quite a while, transferring me, bit by bit until my
octopus form was fully out of the box. Then I used my
avatar's camouflage ability to match the coloring
around me, as I moved slowly toward the corner of the
table. If I moved too quickly, my camouflage wouldn't
be able to match my background well and I'd appear
like a blur. This way, I remained as hidden as possible
as I reached the corner then grappled down a leg. Once
I was on the floor, I reverted to my human form. I could
still use my avatar's camouflage and did so, keeping
myself blended in with my surroundings. I resisted the
urge to stretch and groan, which I really wanted to do

after being trapped and confined in my avatar form so long.

Again, I moved slowly, speed would only lessen my ability to hide. Inch by inch, I crept to a wall. Then... ponderously slowly. I stood up.

I was directly across the room from the guards, standing there, looking at them, and even though their gaze passed over me... they couldn't see me.

Then, again achingly slowly, I inched my way along the wall to a corner. Then along the next wall to a corner, then along that wall to a place next to where the guards were sitting. I got close to them, then reached out, using my body manipulation to extend one arm, until I could grab them, both at once.

I was in a foul mood and felt the need for haste, so I used my manipulation to seal their mouths and liquify their bones. It was a horrible fate, but I had no mercy for these Thraians. They both collapsed into writhing piles of muscle. I dropped my camouflage and grabbed the keys from the belt of one of the guards, then unlocked my friends.

Falcon flew out and veered into his human form, groaning and stretching as I had wanted to do.

Rhino buzzed out of his caged and did the same. I could see the rage in the large man's eyes.

"We need to keep quiet!" I hissed as Rhino looked like he was about to pick up the table and smash it against a wall in his frustrated fury.

He quivered with rage but seemed able to control

himself. Those green eyes of his smoldered as he nodded to me, jaw clenched tight.

The door to our room opened and we all spun to see... someone. I didn't recognize him, but he was dressed in finery, not armor, and he wasn't Demir.

"Oh good, you're free. That will help."

"Who are you and why shouldn't we kill you?" Falcon growled.

The man smiled and nodded. "An understandable reaction. I am Prince Ensar, and I wish to help my brother, Lyran."

"He didn't mention you," I said suspiciously. I wasn't going to trust any of these princes.

"He doesn't know about me. It's a long story, which we don't have time for. I came here to free you and your Lady. Demir is on his way to her now, and I fear for what he will do to her. You don't need to trust me. I understand if you don't. If I lead you astray, my life is forfeit, will that do for now?"

Rhino rushed to the man, pushing him back out the door, large hand around the man's neck, lifting him with ease to pin him high against the wall of the hall outside. Falcon and I followed.

"I think your terms are agreeable," I said, hoping Rhino didn't kill the man right away. "If this is some elaborate trap, Rhino there will rip you limb from limb. Deal?"

The prince nodded.

"That way!" he said, voice strained, pointing. "To the

stairs at the end of the hall, then down a level and... well it would be easier and faster if I could take you there."

I still didn't know if I could trust this man, but... "Rhino, let him down. Transform and stay on his shoulder. If he betrays us, you can do what you like to him."

Rhino hesitated, then did as asked. He dropped Ensar and veered into beetle form, flying up to land on the prince's shoulder. Ensar led the way. We followed, and I prayed this man was here to help us... because I'd never forgive myself if anything happened to Roo.

CHAPTER 4

ROO

THE WORST PART OF MY IMPRISONMENT WAS KNOWING I could escape at any time. If I veered into my avatar form, I'd be free of these manacles and could easily slip from this room to search these dungeons for my men. But... if I didn't find them before someone realized I was missing... they might die. And I couldn't live with that. So, I lay there, cold and desolate.

But I was far from inactive.

If I could locate Rhino, Ceph, and Falcon using my emotional connection to them, perhaps then I'd be able to escape from this room and free them.

Demir had found out about my emotional-push, but I doubted he knew of my deep connection with my guys. Even if he did, I didn't think there would be any way to block that link. So, I reached out through my emotions. I'd spent several months with the three men now, which was the longest I'd spent with anyone since I'd acquired my spirit-gift. I felt a deep connection to them and knew I could find them.

I didn't even have to reach out that far before I found them. They were moving... toward me. Did that mean they were free or just being moved? I didn't know and didn't care. If they were still captive, I'd free them somehow.

Yet... even as I retracted my empathy, I snagged on a particularly strong snarl of emotions also headed my way and much closer: lust and sadism.

Demir was coming and he was nearly here, just outside, in the hall.

I made a split-second decision. I'd been planning on veering into my kangaroo rat form and just scurrying out of here, but if I did and Demir arrived at an empty cell, he might get to my guys before I did. I couldn't risk that. So, I did veer, but only for a split second before returning to myself. That got me out of my shackles. I kept my hands and feet roughly where they had been though, so hopefully no one would notice.

Now... I would play a very dangerous game with Demir.

Calm yourself, you can defeat this bastard, Leoa said softly within me. *You are a master of spirit and emotions, use that. Even if he may be stronger than you are physically, I know you can defeat him.*

I will, I must. I forced down any lingering fear and anxiety and found a certain... purposeful peace.

Then the door to my cell opened.

Luckily Demir carried no torch. With the cell still dark he might miss that my ankles and wrists were no longer chained. Certainly, I sensed he had other things on his mind. His lust was a throbbing, putrid cloud, which filled the room around me.

He wore only a silken robe, which he slid off and handed to someone just outside the cell, commanding them: "Hold this." Then, I watched his obese silhouette approach.

"Are you ready for me, my naughty little whore?" he whispered.

I bit back the words I wanted to shout at him. I needed him closer for my plan to work. "Come closer, master," I said. The words burned upon my tongue.

"Yes, it seems you are willing." He giggled with glee.

Only then did I see the small knife he held, light flashing off the blade. That would complicate things, but... might also help in the end, if I could do this right.

As he drew closer, I saw his beady eyes and, as I'd hoped, they weren't looking at my hands or feet, but... everything else in between. I suppressed a shudder at that.

Calm, Leoa reminded me, helping to instill the emotion as the time for action drew near.

Demir knelt next to me, raising the knife. "Time for some foreplay," he said with a manic grin.

That was close enough.

I'd learned from my last attack on his emotions that fear only caused him to lash out with his pain ability. So instead, I drained all of his emotions away, leaving only a touch of befuddled confusion in a blank void.

He swayed, eyes unfocused for a moment.

I quickly spun, drawing my legs up, then kicked with both feet, using all the strength of my enhanced leaping ability to smash Demir in the face.

He was thrown back, dropping his knife.

I leapt to my feet, plucking up the knife, then raced across the cell to Demir. As I did, I reached out to whoever was outside and drained their emotions as well, so they'd be stunned for a moment and wouldn't come in or call out.

I knelt next to the stunned form of Demir, feeling just a little satisfaction at his shattered nose and lips, leaking blood. I put the small knife to his throat but hesitated. I hated to kill any living thing; and Demir still vaguely qualified as a 'thing.' The blade was only a couple inches long, but it would cut deep enough to kill him if I sunk it into his neck.

But... could I do it?

No. Even with all he'd done to me, I couldn't bring myself to take his life.

Luckily, I didn't have to.

I sensed that my men were arriving!

"No! Wait!" The voice startled me. I didn't recognize it. I looked to see a fourth man with my guys. In the dimness of the dungeon, I didn't recognize him, and his voice hadn't sounded familiar.

But Ceph's voice was, and it was a balm on my soul to hear him: "Roo! Oh, thank all the Spirits!"

I shoved more confused emptiness into Demir, to make sure he didn't recover from this stunned state. Then I took a moment to just... take in my wonderful men! Rhino, massive and strong, held the jailer by his neck like some doll. Falcon was poised for action watching the hallway. Ceph was rushing to me, filled with concern and love.

And that other man... now that I had a moment to sense him with my emotions... I did indeed recognize him. He felt similar to someone I'd scanned before... One of the princes, the second oldest... Ensar? What was he doing here?

"Don't kill him," Ensar said. "I have other ways of making him forget all about this, but if you kill him my brothers will come after you, hunt you down. If we leave him, most of them won't care that much that you've escaped. I can keep them from coming after you."

"Why would you do that?" I asked, hearing the harsh bitterness in my voice. With everything I'd been through I was not in a trusting mood.

Then Ceph was gathering me up into a tight embrace, squeezing me as if both of our lives depended on how tightly he held me.

"Spirits, I... I thought..." He looked down at Demir and the knife in my hand. "Apparently, I shouldn't have been too worried. Of course you can free yourself!"

I wanted to tell him he was right to have been

worried, but that would have only added to his apprehension. Instead, I was more concerned about Ensar.

"Why are you helping us? This is a trap." My tone was clearly accusing. Ceph released me, and I knelt next to Demir again. Once before, I had felt revulsion and hatred so visceral it had forever changed me. That had been after Swan's attack as we'd left Elista. I felt that same abhorrent emotion grip me now. And as much as I could not kill, I was filled with this need to exact some price upon this man who had been so vile and disgusting. And suddenly my mind filled with exactly how I could do it. "I won't kill him," I hissed. "But... I will emasculate him. That seems just." Yes, that was exactly what he deserved.

I sensed shock from all four men.

"I..." Ensar stammered a few things which weren't words, then... "Dragon's Teeth..." that seemed like some sort of curse. "Yes, do it. The man's a lecherous pig who thrives on hurting people. It seems a fitting punishment."

"How's this for pain," I whispered to Demir as I grabbed his limp cock and with a flick of the knife, removed it at the base.

Demir screamed, eyes going wide as I threw his cock across the cell.

Ensar rushed in and put a hand to the other prince's head, then Demir blinked, seeming confused.

Ceph was there a moment later as well. He too touched Demir and the man's wound healed leaving the stub of a cock. At the same time, Demir's balls shriveled up and fell off. I guessed that was Ceph's work as well. Good, I hadn't wanted to touch that.

I stood slowly, with a grim smile, even as I felt sick within. I couldn't quite believe I'd done that, and at the same time it had felt so very right. Even so, I was trembling.

You've been through a lot; you're starting to feel the effects of that now, Leoa said, and I felt comfort and reassurance from her.

Falcon came to me, putting a robe over my shoulders, covering me. I pulled it tight around me as I looked at the dumbfounded Demir. I felt Falcon close behind me. Strong arms wrapped around me, and I pressed myself into his warmth and the comfort of his embrace as I began trembling. I was finally allowing myself to feel the fear I'd been repressing.

"What did you do?" I asked Ensar. Curious why Demir looked so... blank, now. A tiny, sadistic part of me had hoped he'd scream just a little longer.

The prince looked up at me. "My dragon-gift is hard to explain, but I can summon The Void. It's like a hungry... nothingness. I am instilling that into Demir's mind, erasing his memories. He'll remember who he is and other elements about himself, but not who you are. I cannot give him new memories, only remove existing ones."

Intriguing.

"How will you explain what happened to him?" Ceph asked.

He shrugged. "I'll say I found him like this, and that I erased his memories to save him the pain of what happened. None of our other brothers will care."

"How... how can you live with these monsters?" I asked, disgusted.

I saw his jaw tense as he looked away, clearly ashamed. "It isn't easy." He sighed. "I was like them once, long ago." He looked up at me and there was something in his eyes. I felt the love in his soul; not for me, but for another. "Then I married the princess of Vorea and... slowly, she changed me. It's too long a story to tell here, but I've come to see that Lyran was right. The empire is corrupted, heart and soul. Things need to change."

"Does that mean you want to come with us?" Falcon asked, his tone clearly suggesting he didn't like that idea.

"No, I will stay here. I need to calm the other princes after your escape and keep an eye on Demir here. But I feel that soon Lyran's rebellion will cause all the princes to act, to fly out to meet him. When they do, at the right time, I will turn on my brothers to aid you."

I still didn't quite believe any of what the man was saying, but I couldn't deny the emotions he was feeling: sorrow, love, shame, grief, even hatred whenever he spoke of his brothers. Not to mention the admiration he felt for Lyran.

"How do we get out of here?" I asked. "And where can I get some clothes?"

Ensar nodded. "Follow me."

"Not without knowing where you're taking us," I said firmly.

He rose. "I'm taking you to my wife. She will be your way out of the palace as well as provide some new clothes for you."

"Our deal remains the same," Ceph said, voice level. "If we even think you're betraying us, you're dead."

I felt Ensar's emotions. As much as I didn't trust him, I knew he felt beholden, ashamed. I didn't think he'd betray us.

Fascinating.

He led the way. Stopping at each person we met — the jailer being the first — to wave his hand at them. They would blink and stand there as if stunned. "They will not remember us passing," Ensar said.

We moved quickly out of the dungeons into — what I guessed were — servant's corridors, narrow and windowless. These we followed for some time. Ensar explained: "It is some distance from Demir's section of the palace to mine."

I was weary in body and soul, unable to walk for long. Rhino plucked me up into his arms and carried me, cradled like a child. I felt warm and safe pressed to that massive chest. My emotions flowed freely then, I wept and shivered, my stomach roiling. Then, I simply felt exhausted.

I must have dozed, as I woke on a soft surface, reclining, covered in a blanket. I was in a massive open area with a great bank of windows along one wall. My guys were close by. Falcon sat on the end of the long divan, on which I rested. Ceph and Rhino were on the floor on either side of me. I sat up slowly.

They came to me. Falcon slid over and held me in strong arms, pulling me close. Kissing the top of my head. Rhino shifted closer, still on the floor, rubbing my legs.

"Drink this," Ceph said, taking a cup from a nearby table and handing it to me. My hands were still trembling when I took it. The liquid was sweet and flavorful, I consumed it all and felt stronger once I had. Ceph watched me intently and I felt his tension ease as I slowly relaxed and stopped shaking.

"We're in the prince's suite," Ceph said looking around. "He left to gather some supplies for our escape, but his wife is... here." He'd paused because his words had seemed to summon the woman. She walked into the large living area with an armful of clothes. A tall woman in her mid-thirties, who possessed white-blonde hair and unyielding, steel-blue eyes.

She nodded to me. "I am Lusine, and I'm so sorry for what's happened to you," she said, setting the clothes down on a nearby chair. "Demir is... a horrible man. I never liked the way he looked at me." She shuddered. "If you ask me, he should have been gelded long ago." She took a moment to smooth her dress. "Ah, now, on to more pleasant matters. I've brough out some items you can try, though I fear you are a bit shorter and fuller of figure than I am. Some of these may be a little snug or too long."

I nodded. "Thank you," I said softly.

A pained expression crossed her face. "It is the least Ensar and I can do. We are... trapped here in many ways, doing the best we can to help others, even if only one person at a time. It isn't much, but it's something." She gave a tight-lipped nod. "I'll leave and let you change."

"Wait," I said curious. "Is what Ensar said true? Did you... change him?"

A soft smile spread onto her lips. "Yes." Perhaps seeing my curiosity, she sat. "I sacrificed myself for my country. I agreed to the marriage only if none of my people were harmed, there would be no conscription and no slaves taken. My kingdom was small, and it didn't harm his reputation much to agree to my demands, so it was settled. After that, I made it my duty to see if there was any good in this man I'd married. We were both a little surprised to find there was. He'd always had a good heart but had hidden it, even from himself. Over time we discovered who he really was, and together we've planned a path for us." Her smile grew. "He brags to this brothers that his harem is the largest of any of them, but... that's only because we've taken those girls in so they wouldn't end up with his brothers. We go together to see them, and we learn about them and their cultures and lands. When possible, like we'll do with you today, we try to smuggle one or two out to return to their lives if they can. He's become the man I hoped he was, and I love him, dearly." Her expression darkened. "My greatest fear is that his brothers will find out what we're doing. It is only his gift of *The Void* which protects him. His older brother, Ati Kaan can read minds and see the truth of people. That's how they'd known your true intentions. But Ensar protects us, all of us, with his *Void*." For the first time I saw a crack in the woman's carefully maintained exterior. "If that fails, so many will suffer."

That explained a lot.

Lusine rose and excused herself again.

I stood, feeling sturdier now. I didn't get far before my guys were all around me, pressing close.

"We…" Falcon began but couldn't go on. I sensed their shame at not being able to protect me, even as I felt their devotion surging strong.

"I know," I whispered. "But we have survived and will continue to survive." I kissed Falcon softly, lingering until I felt his shame begin to melt away with the warmth of our love. Then I pulled Ceph down to do the same, and despite the others still pressing close, he slipped arms around me to hold me tight as we reassured each other through the connection of our joined lips. And when Ceph was sated, Rhino plucked me up and we kissed. He, of all of them, had felt the shame of capture the most. A part of his soul still hadn't healed from Swan's attack, where he'd nearly died protecting me. I felt his desperate need to be stronger, tougher, surer. When I pulled back from our kiss, I whispered to him. "You are everything to me; everything I need."

"And you are everything to us," Ceph breathed.

"I will never fail you again," Rhino said, full of uncertain conviction. I felt he wouldn't believe his own promise until he'd been able to carry it out.

"There is nothing we won't do for you," Falcon finished.

I drew in a long breath. "Then... help me find some clothes," I said and that helped to dissipate the tension we all felt.

I checked the dresses and indeed, few of them would fit me. I selected a rather baggy, cream-colored dress, which was meant to be worn with many straps of cloth to adjust it to a woman's figure. I used only one strip, as a belt. I also took a white cloak.

Not long later Ensar returned, carrying several bits of armor and weapons. He'd had to guess about sizes — and fitting anything to Rhino had been out of the question — so we made up Ceph and Falcon to look like palace guards as best we could.

He explained his plan: Lusine often went into the city, escorted by two guardsmen. She would do so again today. Ceph and Falcon would be her guards, and Rhino and I would veer into our avatars to travel in small pouches. Ensar had dispatched two guards to ride hard to the meeting place and wait for his wife. They would escort her home again. It would seem like nothing had changed.

Once we were ready, Lusine embraced Ensar, and I could feel the intensity of the bond between them, the strength of their love.

Then we were on our way. At first light, Lusine took a carriage down into the city. Her first stop was at an inn nearly all the way across the city. Lusine gave us a heavy bag of gold and bade us farewell. "There is a hostler and an outfitter not far down the road and a seamstress nearby as well. This should buy you anything you need. I wish you luck," she said. Then she was back in her carriage and off with the two planted guards.

None of us wanted to linger in the capital, so we didn't stop for horses or clothes. We hurried out of the city on foot, getting only enough food and provisions to last us until we reached the next city. There, we'd outfit ourselves properly.

We were finally free.

CHAPTER 5

DAWN

It was a small force of Njorvasoturi that I brought back to Noora Kyla with me. More than half of their Karhukora riders had been sent in various directions to begin gathering the other clans. That left four of the great beasts and twenty of the stout northerners. I hoped we might still make a difference, if the Thraians returned north to attack the village we'd liberated.

Our trip north — following the markers Eiva had found — had been slow. We'd been moving carefully to keep an eye out for the signs. That meant the trip south — riding the Karhukora — took less than a full day. We'd set out before dawn and were now drawing close to Noora Kyla as evening set in.

That's when Swift found us.

The bird dove from the sky, veering as it began to slow, and Swift dropped to the ground before me. "Oh, thank the Spirits! Lyran is hurt, dying, and there is a force of Thraian approaching the town, but—"

He was cut off by a light blooming in the south, beyond the village and a moment later we all heard the accompanying roar.

"Eophon is dealing with them," Swift finished. "I couldn't stop them after Lyran was hurt. Delaying them until now was the best I could do. We need to make sure none of the Thraians return south to report this." He quickly added, "Lyran is still alive, for now, but I don't know how long he has." Swift was desperate. The situation seemed dire indeed.

It was a lot to take in, but my mind assimilated the information quickly. I turned to Astraed. "Do you have healers among you?"

"I am one, but—"

I didn't care about any conditions, if she could help, I'd take her to Lyran. I spun back to Swift.

"Swift, this is Mauno," I introduced the two quickly. "Take them to the battle, perhaps they can help with the clean-up afterward." To Mauno: "I trust Swift with my life, follow him please." Then back to Astraed: "I'm sorry for this indignity." Then I picked her up — the advantage of being stronger than I looked — and leapt as far as my empowered jumps would take me, hopping quickly over the countryside.

Astraed had tried to protest, but then had quieted, clinging to me desperately.

It was only as I reached Noora Kyla, that I realized I

hadn't asked Swift where Lyran was. I paused only for a moment and concentrated. I wasn't as innately connected to him as I was to Roo, but I hoped I could sense him. I spread out my spirit-gift to try to reach him.

"Dawn, please—" Astraed tried.

"Hush," I said.

And she did.

My spirit-gift was meant for relatively close, tactical use: sensing every little shift in the people and environment around me to tell me what was happening. I'd never stretched it as far as I did now.

I think this will work, Amya said, lending me power. *Concentrate on Lyran. Your gift knows him, knows his scent and form. Seek that, use your connection to him, your love.*

I did as instructed and filled the countryside around Noora Kyla with my gift. I sensed the battle: the fire pouring down from the sky and the chaos of the troops. I sensed Swift, Pan, Mauno and the other Njorvasoturi rushing south. I sensed... another force at the edge of the forest. Some of them were attacking any of the Thraians who tried to flee.

And that is where I found Lyran.

"Hold on," I whispered to Astraed and leaped again.

Ten more bounding cross-country leaps and I was at Lyran's side.

"Please," I begged Astraed. "Do what you can for him," I said this even as my gaze fully took him in. "Spirits," I breathed. "No." He was far too still, laying wrapped tight in bandages, including his face. Far too much of the white cloth was stained heavily with red. He looked like he was already in his burial shroud. Yet, if he was still bleeding, he was still alive. At least I hoped that was so.

"That's what I tried to tell you," Astraed said sternly. "My healing requires balance, a give and take. I am just a conduit. I must borrow life from another to restore one who is wounded."

"Then take from me!" I insisted. "Please!" I knelt next to Lyran and touched one small exposed area of skin. I sent my spirit-gift into him. I hadn't done this before, but I felt it was possible: using my gift to see how hurt he was.

I cringed at the wrongness I felt within him; so much pain and damage. Even worse than the external injuries were the internal wounds: blood moving where it shouldn't, organs failing, heart slowing. "Please!" I begged Astraed again. "Do it now! Take from me!"

She knelt next to me. "Are you certain?" she asked, concerned. "If he is near death, he may require more than you can give. It may kill you to try to save him."

"Just do it!" I cried. "What do you need me to do?"

She sighed and relented. "Lie next to him."

I did, and she knelt between our heads. Her hands moved over me in a swirling, mixing dance, moving slowly upward. I felt stirrings within me, my body responding to what she was doing. Her hands fell and the dance began again, and this time I felt a pull. I gasped as strength and energy, what felt like the literal life within me was swept up and out. And above me, around her hands, lights began to swirl. It was a waving, shimmering dance of colors, smoldering reds and hot oranges, bright yellows and burning whites, all the colors of fire. And those lights grew in size and intensity of color as more of me was drawn up into them. Then the pull stopped, and I could finally catch my breath. Astraed kept her hands swirling, as if keeping the lights under control with her movements, as she shifted and moved the colorful display over Lyran. Then the process happened in reverse and the lights dimmed and went out as — I guessed — she was pushing energy into the man to heal him.

But she was shaking her head. "He is very far gone. That has sustained him, kept him from fading further, but nothing more. I'll need to draw more from you."

Spirits. I already felt like I'd been trampled by a herd of horses. But I couldn't let Lyran die.

"Take whatever you need," I said, surprised at how weak my voice sounded. Though, perhaps I shouldn't have been.

"I sense... something else inside you, another... entity?" Astraed seemed confused but pushed on. "Might I take energy from this as well?"

Amya was quick to answer. *Yes, of course.*

"Yes," I said. "Do what you must."

Her swirling dance of hands began again. I felt my essence being pulled out of me. The fiery lights grew and danced and swirled and I nearly passed out as she finished her draw from me. I could feel Amya weakening as well.

That was... intense. I haven't felt this weak in... well... ever.

I didn't even have the capacity to think a response to him. My world was swirling as well, darkness hovering at the edges of my vision. I too had never quite felt this weak before. Once, as a child, I'd had a terrible fever and everything had been as swimming and delirious as it was now, but this somehow felt even worse.

Astraed moved my energy over to Lyran and again it dissipated ever-so-quickly into him.

"Take... more..." I rasped, barely able to form words.

"You'll die." Astraed was shaking her head.

"Don't care... Save him!" I gasped.

"As you wish," she whispered and began again. And this time, I did not make it even to the end. I blacked out as those lights were still growing and swirling.

Dawn? Amya seemed to be calling from some great distance. *Dawn? Don't slip away!*

But I was afloat in a cold darkness and everything, including Amya seemed removed and insignificant as I floated farther and farther from it all.

Dawn no! But even that was just a whisper.

Then... nothing.

CHAPTER 6

PAN

I rushed to Dawn's side as Astraed, the Njorvasoturi elder, pulled what seemed the last of Dawn's essence out of her. I wasn't even sure what was happening, but that seemed to describe what I was seeing: the pull of brilliant colors from Dawn's body.

Dawn went limp, and I gasped a cry.

Astraed, tight-lipped and pale, moved the energies she'd captured over Lyran, and they dissipated quickly into him.

"Is Dawn...?" I couldn't finish.

"She hangs by a thread," Astraed said. "I have taken all I can from her, perhaps too much."

"Then take from me," I hissed quickly. I didn't even know what that meant, I just knew I had to help Dawn. "Save her, save Lyran, do what you must, please!"

Astraed nodded. "It is clear to me now how much you

all care for each other: such love and devotion. Lie down here." She indicated a spot, and I did.

Then Astraed began doing what she'd been doing to Dawn over me, and I felt the strangest sensation of my very life-force being pulled out from me.

"There is another entity within you too," Astraed said, shaking her head. "Very odd. Can I take from it as well?"

Yes, of course, Eona said to me. *We cannot let Dawn, nor Lyran, die.*

"Yes!" I relayed the message.

Astraed pulled more and I felt Eona's corresponding gasp of surprise.

Astraed moved her hands over Dawn and some of the swirling mass of colors — different from what she'd pulled from Dawn, mine seemed to be darker: black, amethyst, dark red — infused down into my love. Dawn gasped once, but then was far too still once again. I didn't know what that meant and Astraed seemed confused as well, lips pursed. She moved the remainder of my energy over Lyran and poured it into him.

She repeated this process again, taking from me to give a little to Dawn and most to Lyran. Dawn didn't change, seeming too pale, too still.

Then Astraed sighed and sat back heavily. "I have done what I can. The other man will live, though he may still be some time recovering. As for Dawn..." She shook her head.

"What? What happened?" I was gasping, so very weak, but I had the strength for this, I needed to know.

Astraed sighed. "Her body is well, but her spirit... I sense it has... retreated. I fear I may have taken too much from her initially. I have tried to restore some of her energies, but it seems to have done little."

"Then take more from me, do what you must to bring her back!" I insisted.

Astraed shook her head. "No, you don't understand. There is nothing I can do now. I have given her enough energy for her body to survive, but it is up to her to return her soul to her body. It is out of my hands. I'm sorry."

"No," I whimpered. My jaw went tight as tears welled up, falling down my cheeks into my ears.

Dawn is strong, Pan, she'll find her way back. I've never known anyone as powerful in spirit as she is. She'll be well. She'll find her way back. Do not worry. Eona was trying to reassure me, but she too was weak and struggling and I felt her uncertainty. Neither of us knew anything about this strange Njorvasoturi healing method and what it might have done to Dawn.

So, I lay there, not strong enough to do much else. It was a challenge to even lift my arm so that I could reach over and grab Dawn's hand. It felt cooler than it should. I squeezed it and prayed to The Great Mother for Dawn's safe return to us.

Sometime later Swift arrived. He said the Thraians were dealt with. A group of roughly sixty of them had surrendered. They were all that had survived. With Lyran and Dawn gone, it was up to Swift and me — and a few of the village elders — to determine what to do with these prisoners. Astraed sat in on our meeting, which took place on the ground around me since I still couldn't move.

Fey revered life, so I was opposed to killing these people. And we all knew we couldn't set them free. So... we decided to give them a choice. They could join us, join Lyran's army, or face Eophon's fires. Wisely, they all decided to switch sides. As it turned out, only a few of the commanders — all of whom were now dead — were actually Thraians. Those with us now were a mix of peoples from other captive kingdoms south of here. They'd been conscripted and forced to fight, and many of them were happy to turn on their former 'allies.'

After a day, I could walk... with help.

After two, I was moving on my own, though still feeling drained.

After three, I was mostly well, but Lyran and Dawn had yet to wake up. Lyran's wounds were closing up well, and the hope was he'd be up and around in another week or so. Yet, Dawn's spirit had yet to return. I stayed by her, whenever I had a free moment, lying next to her, stroking her hair and rubbing her skin, which seemed far too cold. I hoped Dawn would gain some strength from me being close, even though Astraed said there was nothing I could do. Still, I loved this small wonder of a woman, and I gave her everything I could give. Yet, her condition didn't change.

Swift and I did what we could, though mostly we waited to see how many of the other Njorvasoturi clans came south. After a week, three clans had joined us, an additional hundred-and-twenty men and women, with thirty-five Karhukora. This included seven males. I'd been a bit surprised to learn all of the large beasts I'd seen so far, were female. The males were monstrous things a third again as large. But they were harder to control and had to be kept away from the females. Added to this were the sixty ex-Thraian Army members. Also, everyone from Noora Kyla would come with us, including the elderly and the young. They weren't all warriors, but they saw no reason to stay here. The village would be abandoned.

There had been a day of mourning for those from the village who had been lost. Many trees were felled, and hundreds of pyres were lit to send off the fallen, both from our side and the enemy.

We'd wait a little longer to see if more Njorvasoturi came, but already we had a force to be reckoned with. The trouble was, we didn't know what to do with this newfound army. Dawn and Lyran had been leading us, and with them still unconscious we were all a little lost.

CHAPTER 7

SWIFT

Two weeks had passed since we'd left Noora Kyla. Lyran was up and about, mostly recovered from his injuries. Dawn however, remained far too still on a bed of blankets in the back of a wagon, even more pale than usual, seeming dead. Astraed assured us her body was well, and we could feel a strong pulse at her neck, but... other than that she was dead to the world. And Astraed was concerned that, without her soul, her body may eventually just... stop.

Once Lyran had awoken, we'd debated what to do and had decided to keep moving ahead with our plans. We would liberate the North.

Only one more clan of Njorvasoturi had joined us before we'd left the north, a small one with six Karhukora and a score of warriors. Still, every one of those men was worth two average fighters and their Karhukora were invaluable.

We'd traveled south, liberating every village we'd come to, making sure no Thraians escaped to warn of a dragon in the north. In fact, many of the Thraians had joined us. Of the Njorvan people, some had chosen to stay and rebuild towns and villages, but some had joined up with us and we now had over two hundred Njorvan warriors, not to mention dozens of refugees — the elderly and young — who travelled with us as well.

And now the time had come for our first real test of this new army. We'd come to Njorva. The once capital of these northern lands and firmly in the grip of the Thraians. An army of five thousand men held the city, and they had strong walls to hide behind if needed, though a portion of the walls to the south were still being rebuilt from their invasion. We had an army of roughly a hundred and fifty Njorvasoturi with forty Karhukora, about two hundred ex-Thraian Army members, and two hundred Njorvans. We also had Pan, myself, Lyran, and Eophon. We considered this a roughly equal fight. The trick would be getting the army out from behind the walls of the city, so our war didn't do any more damage to the buildings and people of Njorva. There was a large area of farmland outside the city to the north which — though it wouldn't be good for the farmers — would make an excellent battlefield. We'd spent the last few days sneaking scouts down to those farms to get the people out to safety.

Now... I was at the head of an army of two hundred men and women — a mix of ex-Thraians and liberated

Njorvans — moving down onto those fields, with drums and horns blatantly announcing our arrival. Our plan was simple. Such a small force as this had no chance against the Thraians and we and they would both know it. If we'd been a large force, they might have stayed behind their walls and let us try to siege them, but as it was... they would probably feel safe bringing most, if not all their army out in a show of force to crush this "pitiful uprising."

Lyran said it all depended on the commander here and how smart or arrogant he was. We quickly found out... he was arrogant, not smart, as the city disgorged — what looked like — their entire army. Eophon, flying unseen above us, relayed the news to me. We'd done it, they were nearly all out of the city.

I couldn't decide if what came next was 'the hard part' or 'the fun part.' My heart was racing, as I faced down an army over twenty times our size.

They sounded their advance.

My force was to feign fear and cowardice, breaking apart and fleeing. It didn't take much acting to do that. We retreated, seemingly in chaos, back up the road. Once off the farmlands, there was only a narrow patch of cleared land to either side of the road, forest dominating everything else.

The Thraians followed us, as planned.

Then, as they funneled into that narrower area of cleared land, three things happened. First: behind our fleeing force and ahead of their charging force, a line of men and woman surged onto the road from the forest, creating a shield wall. Our force then quickly turned around to reinforce them. Second: at the back of the Thraian lines, fire began pouring down from the sky as Eophon joined the fight. He was the hammer, forcing the Thraians onto the anvil of our shield wall. Third: from either side of the Thraians, Njorvasoturi on Karhukora came charging out of the forest to plow through the confused middle of the Thraians, crushing them from either side.

It was executed flawlessly and what should have been an easy victory for the Thraians turned into a rout as their lines collapsed, men panicking.

By sunset, the city had surrendered. Eight-hundred ex-Thraians joined our army. The small force remaining in the city had tried to flee south, but we had also planned for that. A small force of our own had ambushed them on the road south of the city, ensuring no one had been able to get away. For all intents and purposes, we had freed the nation of Njorva.

We stayed in the city for almost a week, resting while long-range scouts sought farther south, to make sure no retaliation was on its way. Everything they found suggested no one knew the north had been liberated. As we lingered, another five hundred men and women emerged from the lands around the capital. They had been fighting their own resistance and joined up with us.

Though we were sad to lose her, Fria, the strongest of the Njorvan warriors from Noora Kyla would stay behind here in Njorva along with a combined force of eight hundred Thraians and Njorvans. They would hold the city and begin guerilla tactics to free the rest of the North. The rest of us, would head back to Lyran's camp in the Maraslad Forest with a force of roughly a thousand men including the fearsome Njorvasoturi.

The liberation of the North was a feat worth celebrating... but Lyran, Pan, and I couldn't join the others in revelry. Not while Dawn remained in her near-death slumber.

"How is she?" I asked Astraed as I entered the room that had been set aside for Dawn. Pan was there, lying next to the Fey woman. Lyran paced the length of the room.

The Njorvasoturi elder rose from checking on Dawn. "Her spirit is still distant, and I fear her body is starting to... fade. I have taken some essence from the ever-willing Pan to help sustain her." The hardened old woman sighed. "If she doesn't return soon..." She shook her head.

My heart constricted, throat tightening. For a moment I couldn't breathe. Lyran spun on Astraed, rage in his eyes, but he didn't say a word. He knew this wasn't Astraed's fault. But his fury simmered with no outlet so he went to the window and bellowed his pain out into the night.

"Thank you," I whispered to Astraed when I found my voice.

She nodded and left.

I went and sat on the bed. Pan roused from an exhausted sleep. "Dawn?"

"No, just me."

He frowned and rolled over to curl up next to her. His pain was evident as well, in the sour and near-silent funk which permeated him.

I rubbed his back. "She'll return to us."

Pan grunted. I don't think he believed me. I wasn't sure *I* believed me.

I reached over Pan to brush some of Dawn's raven hair off her pale-as-death face. My heart ached to see those luminous golden eyes once more.

I needed her to live.

I... needed her.

You mustn't lose hope! Isoa tried to sooth me, but I felt they were just as concerned and uncertain as I was.

As long as she's alive there's hope. That had become my mantra. It helped that I could feel my twin, somewhere far to the south. He was doing well. His spirits had lifted recently. He was heading north, which was just a guess, but I felt it to be true, though I couldn't say how or why. The fact that he was well and in high spirits helped me to maintain my own. Still, Dawn's stillness ate away at all of us.

Later that week, we departed for the Maraslad forest, a month's journey. I ached to see my brother again, and Roo. I found it so fascinating that two women — who couldn't be more different — had so captured my heart. Dawn was small, slight, and pale, fearsome and reckless.

Roo was a full-figured woman with tawny skin and a large heart, compassionate and caring. Though, in truth, I knew what had drawn me to them: their spirit. Both were women who possessed a powerful presence, which enhanced their outward beauty. The thought of being with both of them at once, was nearly too much to contemplate. But having been with Dawn and the other men who loved her, and seeing how miraculous an event that had been, I began to wonder what it might be like... to have all of us together, Dawn and Roo and all the men who loved them. That would be a joining of such spirit and love I knew it could only be an amazing experience.

So, I tried to think of that, of what I had to look forward to. I tried not to think of what I might lose if Dawn didn't wake.

That... I dared not contemplate... or it might tear me apart.

CHAPTER 8

FALCON

I COULDN'T QUITE MAKE SENSE OF THE SCENE BELOW ME.
Men in boats were trying — and failing — to storm an
island fortress in the middle of a large lake. Was this
some form of practice warfare? We were still within the
borders of the empire. There shouldn't have been any
fighting here.

Unless...

Do you think it's possible? Eluei asked. *Some holdout
kingdom within the borders of the empire?*

*With an island like that, they could probably hold for
some time, but... it just doesn't seem possible.* I was just a little
shocked at this inconceivable sight.

I flew back to the others, who were waiting in a forest
glade well away from the conflict. We'd stopped when
we'd heard the distant sounds of fighting, and I'd gone to
investigate.

Over the past several weeks, we'd been moving

steadily north and east, toward the Maraslad Forest. Travelling on foot and in our avatar forms. We'd learned how to travel quickly as our avatars, using a small pouch. It wasn't comfortable for Roo, Rhino, and Ceph, as they were all bundled inside, but it wasn't too heavy for me to carry as a falcon. Hence, we'd made very good time.

I suppose it was possible we were closer to the fringes of the empire than we'd thought. We only had a rough map of this region of the world, which we'd purchased in our travels. Still, it didn't seem likely. We thought ourselves well south of the northern borders of the empire and far west of the eastern borders.

I landed in the clearing and transformed. "Something's not right," I said quickly. "At first, I thought the Thraians were fighting themselves in some sort of wargame, but if so, they're doing a very good job of killing themselves, which doesn't seem productive. No... I think we've reached some form of hold-out kingdom in the middle of the empire." I saw the shocked looks of the others and quickly explained. "The defenders are on an island, a good sized one in the middle of a large lake. And the entire island is a fortress with solid stone walls. The Thraians have to approach on boats, which are easily burned with fire arrows. Even once they get to the island, there isn't much land outside the walls for them to form a beachhead upon. The attackers are open and defenseless."

"But how long could those defenders hold out without supplies?" Ceph asked.

That is my concern as well, Eluei breathed.

"I think a better question is: how long have they been holding out so far?" Roo said softly. She seemed to be thinking. "From every estimate we have of our travel..." She quickly pulled off her pack and took out the old map we'd purchased. She crouched, spreading it out on the ground, looking at it quickly, then tapped on it. "Yes, I think we've made it much farther than expected. Look I'm guessing we're here at this lake." The map was rough to begin with, a series of lines for roads and rivers and a few towns. The northeast of it was taken up with a forest, which was supposed to be the Maraslad Forest, and just before that was a large lake."

I looked at what she was indicating and tried to compare that with what I'd seen from the air.

What do you think Eluei?

It seems possible, yes, I think Roo's right.

It meant we were much closer to our goal, and I'd soon be able to see my brother and Dawn again. I was a bit desperate to see them both.

Roo sighed, sitting back on her haunches. "I guess the question is, do we stop and try to help these islanders?" She looked up at us. We all knew Roo well enough. She wanted to help. She practically lived to help. That hefty sum of money Lusine had given us had gone toward supplies and clothes — sturdy travel clothes, nothing fancy — but had also been parceled out to the poor and desperate. The fact that we had paid an old man a gold piece for this old map — more than twenty times what it was worth — which barely showed us much of any worth, was testament to how Roo liked to help anyone she could.

The three of us men looked up from Roo to share a knowing look. Yes, of course we'd help... because we all knew that's what she'd do. Ceph put it into words the best. "It couldn't hurt to stop in and see how they're doing."

Roo smiled, rolling up the map and putting it away. "Good." Though she instantly frowned. "I guess this means back in the bag for us though, hunh?"

I shrugged with an I'm-really-sorry grin. The three of them did not much like that means of travel and relished our times walking together.

I got out the small sack and they veered into their avatars, I helped each of them into the sack, then secured it, tying the top. We'd put a few small holes in it, to help with airflow, but they were otherwise trapped. Then I shifted into my falcon and plucked up the bag, flying back out over the lake.

The attack seemed to be done for the day, the boats making their way back to the shore.

There are far fewer boats than what we saw earlier, these defenders certainly seem to know what they're doing. Eluei was impressed.

I circled a little, looking for a good place to set down, spying what looked like a disused pigeon coop. I flew in the wide opening in one side and settled to the floor with the bag. Transforming, I looked around. There were cages here for a score or more of pigeons, but the room was empty and looked long disused. It seemed as good a spot as any to land. I untied the bag and let the others out. They reverted to their true forms as well.

"What now?" Rhino asked.

"Let's go introduce ourselves," Roo said with a friendly smile and walked right out of the room into the rest of the large keep. We moved through several halls, which seemed little used before coming to what seemed like more travelled ways.

Roo was marching along with such purpose that the first few people we passed paid us no mind, but eventually one older man furrowed his brow at us as he passed, and he stopped. "Who are you?" he asked suspiciously.

I almost pitied the man. I knew what he was about to get: the full Roo treatment.

She beamed at him, extended a hand to be shaken, exuding peace and serenity. "I'm Lady Roo of Elista. These men and I are here to help you fight the Thraians."

The man blinked a few times. I knew Roo would be working her magic upon his emotions, helping him along to trusting us. "Who?" he said after a moment. Even then he seemed to unknowingly reach up and take her hand. She gave a formal — if not particularly deep — curtsey and he bowed his head to her.

"Lady Roo of Elista, and this is Lord Ceph, Lord Rhino, and Lord Falcon. We're here to help. Who might we talk to about the best way to be of service to you good people?"

Eluei laughed within me. *It's that blunt but cheerful honesty. No one expects it.*

"I..." the poor old man seemed quite flustered. "I am Senior Chamberlain Jacek of Osera." That seemed all he was capable of saying for a moment. He blinked at us. "How... did you get in here?" he asked slowly as if the entire notion of us being here was impossible. I didn't blame him. These people were well secluded on their island.

"Through the pigeon coop," Roo said as if it happened every day. "I know this must be a bit of a surprise, but we are here to help. We too are at war with the Thraians and... were just passing by your lovely little island here, and we thought—"

"Just... passing by?" Jacek said slowly. "How? Were you flying?" He'd meant it as a sarcastic joke.

"Yes."

Jacek blinked for a while before he finally blew out a breath. "Well, you're not trying to kill me, so that's something. I'll take you to Commander Lucjan. She can figure out what to do with you. Ah... follow me please."

"Thank you, good sir," Roo said with her usual beatific smile. She patted his hand, still holding hers. He looked at her hand then finally released it before turning and walking.

We followed the man up into a tower of the keep. There, at what must have been close to the top, we came up from a set of stairs into a room which encompassed the entirety of the square tower. The stairs continued up farther, but this room was large and wide, with glassed windows along each wall, providing an amazing view of the surrounding lake.

"Ah... Commander Lucjan?" Jacek said a bit uncertain. "It seems we have visitors. This is Lady Roo of Elista, accompanied by Lord's Ceph, Rhino, and Falcon."

"What strange names," said the woman in armor that Jacek had addressed. She was leaning over a table in the middle of the room spread with papers and hadn't looked at us yet. "And sorry, did you say prisoners? From the last raid?"

"Ah... no? They're visitors... They flew here? From..." Jacek turned to us in question.

"Elista, by way of the Thraian capital," Roo said as if it were nothing.

That opened his eyes a little.

And it got Lucjan's attention. She straightened and turned. "You're from the Thraian capital?"

"No, we're from Elista, but we were recently in the capital, gathering information for the rebellion against Thraan, of which we're a part." Roo smiled.

There it is again, blunt, cheerful honesty. Eluei gave the impression of shaking her head, grinning.

The lady-commander blinked. She was tall and squarely built, wearing worn and unadorned armor. Her pale brown hair was a bit mussed up and her brown eyes confused at the moment. "Care to repeat that?" she asked.

Roo smiled, stepping away from the rest of us to curtsey before the commander. "I'm sorry for the confusion. I know this must be hard to understand, but we're from Elista, a nation to the east of here. Thraan is threatening our borders, so we sent an expedition to try to negotiate with them. That was a bad idea it seemed, and we were captured and befriended by a rogue dragon lord, the youngest prince of Thraan, who is working against his family to overthrow the empire. And for him we went to the capital to gather information, where we were promptly secured and harassed, until we castrated one of their princes and another prince helped us escape to return to the east, and on our way back we found you. It's a pleasure to meet you."

The commander's eyes were shifting slowly, as if still assimilating all of what Roo had said. She nodded slowly. "Did you say castrated?"

"Yes."

"Oh…" Lucjan stared at Roo in wonder for a moment. "And how did you get into our keep?" she asked.

"Through the pigeon coop. We flew in. Elistan nobility have the ability to change shape into animals." Roo motioned to me. "Falcon, if you will?"

I veered and flapped over to land on Roo's shoulder.

Lucjan blinked, though surprisingly she didn't seem overly shocked. Instead, her brow was furrowed and she seemed to be thinking. "Yes… I've heard of you. I do recall something in my studies about a nation in the east with nobles who took the forms of animals."

I flew back to the floor and transformed back.

"And what do you wish of me?" the commander

asked. "I do apologize. We're in the middle of a war at the moment and haven't had guests in some time, our hospitality is lacking."

"We want to help," Roo said with a smile. "We wish to see all nations free of Thraian influence. We were surprised to come across your island here. It seemed well within the borders of the empire. How long have you been fighting the Thraians?"

"Almost five years." There was a gruff pride behind those words.

I saw Roo's surprise and it matched mine. "Without help? Without supplies?" Ceph asked.

Lucjan grimaced and nodded. "To a degree yes. We have the lake around us to provide some food, and we have a group of scouts out there on the north-eastern shore, hunting and gathering for us. We send out boats every night to gather what we can from them. But the Thraian patrols of those shores are increasing. Let me show you." Lucjan turned and motioned us over to the table she'd been at when we'd arrived. She leaned far over the table and pulled back a large map. It was of a smaller region than ours, the lake was in the middle of the map, and it had the surrounding areas.

"The Thraians have their main camp here." The commander pointed to what looked like farmlands on the bottom-left corner of the map, south-west. "Before they arrived, our kingdom had many farms and villages out there." Lucjan sighed. "The Thraians have been slowly spreading out from there, but the Maraslad Forest is thick and hard to navigate. It's taken them some time to set up the series of small camps and outposts around the lake to get to the far side. But we believe by the end of this year they'll have secured the lake and we'll be completely cut off from outside help."

"So that *is* the Maraslad Forest?" I asked.

Lucjan's brow furrowed, perhaps sensing from how I'd worded my question that I was aware of the place. "Yes. Why?"

"Help may be closer than you think," Roo said. "We are on our way to meet up with a group of resistance fighters in that forest."

"Where exactly, do you know?"

"Ah... no."

"Then good luck finding them. The Maraslad covers almost a million square miles. And there are few roads through it. It would be a great place for a group of resistance fighters to hide, but if the enemy can't find them, how can you?"

That... hadn't occurred to us. Though... "We have ways," I said. I could feel my brother and I knew Roo could feel Dawn as well. We'd be drawn to them. I shared a look with Roo, and we nodded to each other.

"Well, if you can find them and send us some help, we'd much appreciate it. Our scouts can only get us so much food, and with almost five thousand men and women on the island, we've been on meager rations for some time." Lucjan sighed heavily, lowering her voice. "And I honestly don't know how long we can hold out against the Thraians. They've almost taken the walls twice, just by sheer force of numbers. But they need the boats to get them out here and that's what we target. Yet they seem to be able to build them as fast as we can destroy them. And... once they've cut off our scouts and our supply of food..."

"I can get you more food," I said with a grin. "In my falcon form I can hunt and bring back small game, or even gather supplies in a small bag and lift them back here. It won't be much on any given trip, but I can keep it up all day."

"And you'd do that, for us, stranger?" Lucjan asked.

"We would," Roo said, a sympathetic look at me. She knew I was about to become very busy and very tired.

Are you sure you're up for this? Eluei asked, a bit skeptical.

Roo wants to help, so help I will.

Eluei didn't question that, she knew the depths of my love for Roo.

"At the same time, Rhino and I can slip into the Thraian camp and sabotage their boat building. That will delay things for a while," Ceph said.

Lucjan seemed at a loss for words. "You Elistans are truly a benevolent people. We would greatly appreciate your assistance." She looked past us and beckoned someone with her hand. "Jacek. Will you find these good people a suite of rooms? They need to rest well today and tonight. Tomorrow, it seems they'll be helping us."

And just like that, we'd rejoined the fight.

CHAPTER 9

ROO

The room was magnificent.

We'd told Jacek we didn't need a suite, just a room with a very big bed and perhaps a couch or two. He seemed intrigued but said nothing and found us exactly what we'd asked for. The room held a massive four-poster bed hung with gauzy curtains in a deep red hue. One wall was all windows, the opposite a massive bank of wardrobes and closets. A sitting area with two long couches and a couple chairs occupied the center of the room and out by the windows was a massive fixed tub of porcelain, large enough for Rhino and me to sit in comfortably. The tub was even self-draining. It seemed this keep designed with run-offs for bathing water. There was a door to a small privy as well, with the ability to pull a cord and have water from some reservoir above wash things away.

We'd requested water for a bath and as we waited for

it, we relaxed and reclined on the large cushioned couches.

Are you thinking what I'm thinking? Leoa's voice was hushed, expectant.

Most assuredly, yes. I'd gotten to know Leoa very well in the few months we'd been together now, and she was... very excited about my little harem of men and all the wonderful sensations they could produce for us.

"You're all going to be very busy over the next few days," I said, taking a long moment to look at each of them, catching their gazes, savoring the hungry looks in their eyes. Ceph's clear blue eyes were steady and reassuring. Rhino's dark green eyes were soft and warm. Falcon's dark eyes were hungry and needful. "I should show you how much I appreciate you, before you leave me to go off on your missions."

We had been sitting spread out among the couches and chairs of the sitting area, but once I'd said that, Ceph and Falcon rose and came to join Rhino and I. Rhino slid over and leaned down, reaching to tilt my head back for a deep, hard kiss, making me melt into him. Ceph sat on my other side and began kissing my neck. His deft fingers quickly undid the ties upon the front of the dress, pulling the fabric off a shoulder to kiss there. And wherever he pressed his lips, tingling seeped into me. He was using his gift, stimulating me. The sensations thrilling out from where he kissed to warm my entire being. I was quickly moving from warm with anticipation to hot with need. Falcon knelt on the floor at my feet, kissing my legs as he inched the skirt of my dress up higher and higher. His one hand moved under my dress and a finger began to trace my folds with delicate pressure. I blossomed, opening at his touch, and felt that single finger dip deeper, slipping inside me to wet itself before tracing that moisture over my folds in a delicious dance.

Oh yes! Leoa moaned

I vocalized her pleasure... and my own.

My men didn't stop when servants came with water to fill the tub. I heard the footfalls of several people padding softly. We were giving them quite a show, I was sure, but I didn't want anyone to stop. I was floating in a dream of love, enfolded in strong arms and pressing lips, and I didn't want it to end.

And when the door finally closed Rhino drew back to ask: "Shall we bathe our Lady?"

Oh... yes. I wanted to feel their hands moving over me in the warm waters, cleansing and arousing me.

The others seemed to think this was a good idea as well. I was lifted and taken to the bath. Not only had the tub been filled, but a long brazier had been heaped with coals and additional metal buckets of water had been placed over the heat. I assumed these could be used to refresh and reheat the waters later.

My guys continued their work. I was slowly, sensuously stripped of my dress. Rhino knelt before me, inching my dress down over my chest, pressing his hips to any newly exposed skin. My nipples were engorged and stiff well before he reached them. And when he did suck one of my swollen areolae into his mouth I let out a heavy, body-arching moan. His tongue slicked my rigid peak, concentrating on that exquisitely sensitive bud for some time before inching down the dress on the other side. My anticipation of his pleasuring my other nipple nearly drove me mad.

At the same time, Falcon was behind me, loosening the three built-in belts over the mid-section of the dress, which had cinched it back, tying at the back. He undid them, letting the dress fall loose around me, then he began kissing my neck, shoulders and the tops of my arms as Rhino slowly drew the dress down. Meanwhile his hands gathered up the skirt so he could reach under it, and those strong fingers of his dug into my bottom, kneading my ample curves.

Ceph danced around us, his touches tracing over us, brushing fingers over any exposed skin. And where he touched, skin raised, and people shuddered and sighed. Then he stood next to me and claimed my lips in a long and passionate kiss, our tongues dancing as he had a moment before. Both his hands cupped my face as if I were the only thing in the world for him to focus on.

All this attention was making me burn with desire. Stoking a fire in my core which had become an inferno by the time my dress — *finally* — slipped to the floor.

I stepped into the warm waters of the bath. They had cooled a little since they'd been poured, but I swore my own super-heated body had them boiling again.

Then... I was given a show. My three men stood

before me and slowly disrobed. I watched them with heat in my gaze, savoring each exposed muscle and limb. I pleasured myself gently as I admired their different forms. Falcon was compact and strong, still growing, with dark skin and a ready smile. Ceph possessed of long muscles on a tall and wiry frame with pale skin and that dark tousle of hair. Rhino was big... in every way, with heavy rounded mounds of muscle, tanned skin, and that boyish face with those intense green eyes.

We are so blessed and lucky, Leoa purred.

Indeed.

The guys gathered up soap, cloths, and scrapers and knelt around the tub to tend to me. I was pampered and cleaned, dunking myself under a few times to get the travel-dirt out of my hair. Then Falcon was in the tub with me, back to me. I helped to bathe him, though in the end I was rather ineffectual, focusing most of my efforts on that amazing cock of his. And when he turned, wanting to take me in the bath... I knew it was time to get out.

Ceph and Rhino quickly changed the water and washed themselves, while Falcon pushed me up against a wall, hard body pressing on me, lips on mine, his kisses hot and deep. I knew we were both achingly ready and I hitched a leg up on his hip to give him a hint. His hands slipped down under my thighs and butt, and he lifted me. I wrapped my legs around him as his cock found the quivering wet folds slid into my core, quickly deep inside me. I gasped as he thrusted with desperate need, his lips now covering my breasts with kisses, teeth and tongue playing with the taut nubs of my nipples. I put my hands behind his head, partly to help support myself, partly to urge his face deeper and harder upon my breasts.

I was teetering on the edge of an orgasm as he drove himself into me, but I wanted to feel his release; to come at the same time as him. It had been some time since we'd been together, and his need was palpable. I didn't want him to wait.

"Yes," I whispered to him. "Come, my love!" And I surged his desire and lust.

He cried out with a gasping, wordless breath as he shuddered and I felt his rush within me, the pounding pulse of his cock as it released. I cried out, feeling his heat inside me and his pleasure resonating through my spirit-gift. A powerful orgasm shook through me, and I put my head back against the wall as I rocked myself on him, grinding and seeking to prolong this exquisite moment. "Yes!" I breathed over and over, between heavy, gasping breaths.

Blessed Spirits, that was delicious, Leoa sighed. *It's been far too long since we've had a room... and... a bed...* I sensed her mounting anticipation of our next round, even as Falcon carried me to the bed, laying me down upon the fluffy blankets before he drew out of me.

Ceph came up next to him and touched his shoulder. Falcon gasped as his cock instantly roused, full and hard again. Ceph winked. "You're welcome." Then Ceph lifted a bottle of oil and smiled at me. "Ready for more?"

"Spirits, yes," I gasped.

"Good." He grinned. "I think I know just how to do this." And with that he knelt and began working his mouth over my already loose folds. I shivered with the renewed bliss his lips worked on my already-so-sensitive slit.

His oiled fingers found my other opening and gently rubbed and probed, spreading the slickness over me. It didn't take much. He quickly had two fingers inside me, and I squirmed at that delicate touch of my receptive canal.

Ceph turned back. "Rhino, lie down. Falcon, take over here for a moment, will you?" Ceph moved over to Rhino, now lying next to me. Ceph applied oil to Rhino's massive cock, and I gasped. Was he going to try to get that inside me... inside my rear opening? Blessed Spirits!

But then I couldn't think anymore, as Falcon was pressing his cock into that oiled tunnel and my mind was exploding with ecstasy at the intensity of the sensations as he slowly pressed his thickness deeper into that tight opening. His thrusts were slow now. He'd had his pleasure and was seeking to prolong mine. He was doing an excellent job. His hands worked as well, one upon my breast, pressing and kneading, the other on my folds, finding my clitoris in slow caressing circles.

A little glazed over with pleasure, I lolled my head to one side, watching Ceph stroke more oil onto Rhino's cock and... I blinked, was I seeing that right? Rhino's cock was shrinking? From his monster length and girth, he was becoming just a bit more sensible in size.

Oh, interesting, Leoa quipped. *I must admit I'm slightly disappointed but definitely curious.*

"Whenever you're ready," Ceph said.

I wasn't sure to whom he'd said it, but Falcon pulled out from me, and I gasped. Then he and Rhino were moving me to lie on top of Rhino, my back to the man's stomach and chest. Then I felt the push of Rhino's still-larger-than-average cock into my rear opening. It was slow and careful, but Ceph had apparently known exactly what size he needed to be. I felt ever-so-full, just at the brink of pain, as I clamped down hard upon that heavy, throbbing shaft inside me.

I'd have needed a lot more oil and working up if he'd been full sized, I told Leoa.

And that would be a bad thing? she joked.

No, but this is certainly a lot... easier and gets us to the main event quicker.

You've gone too long without, haven't you? Impatient woman.

Oh, you know you want them all-together too.

Yeah... I do. You're right.

"How is that?" Ceph asked, I felt his hand stroking me, slipping from my wet folds down to caress Rhino's base as well. "Too much? Want... more?"

I was curious. "Perhaps just a bit more?"

Ceph grinned. Rhino, behind me, grunted. "You already feel like you're squeezing me."

Ceph's fingers traced down back to Rhino's cock and the man's erection swelled just a little. Rhino and I gasped together.

"Spirits!" Rhino breathed. I heard him breathing through his teeth, trying to control himself. For my part, I felt so impossibly full. Every twitch of movement — either from me or Rhino — sent shocking thrills through me. These mini-orgasms had me spasming and shuddering even more, which caused more heart-pounding bliss.

Then Ceph was moving up between my legs, opening Rhino's legs as well and pushing his long cock inside my folds, as his hands massaged my thighs and clitoris. He looked over his shoulder at Falcon. "Come on in," he said with a grin. "Just oil me up first."

Falcon grinned.

This man-on-man-on-woman thing was still new for me and Leoa... but we both loved it.

"If you're going to wring me out, it's only fair I do the same," Rhino whispered, voice and body trembling as he reached around me and found my breasts. His large hands were perhaps the only ones which could fully encompass my expansive bosom and he grasped and crushed the sensitive orbs as he began slow thrusts inside me.

I pressed my head into Rhino's chest, back arching. My breath caught and I could hardly breathe. I definitely had no words, only an open-mouthed, gasping need. I was on fire. Every rapid, pounding beat of my heart surged flames through me. My mini-orgasms were gone, and I was shuddering through full-on, heavy releases, climbing a mountain of ecstasy higher and higher.

Ceph wasn't thrusting at all yet, just pressed deep into me as his hands worked miracles. Then he suddenly jerked and thrust deep. I gasped and flared my eyes open to see Falcon's hands lifting my thighs as he thrust hard into Ceph, which had caused the other man to press so deeply inside me. Ceph's expression was of exquisite bliss as he was force-thrusted repeated into me. I sensed his impending climax, the bubbling desire within him before... his body tensed, eyes rolling back, but he didn't release. He was keeping himself him from coming, poised at the peak of his desire as Falcon took him harder and harder.

Rhino began his own quicker strokes, hard and deep. With those two amazing cocks so near inside me, pressing close and thrusting deep, I gave up all pretense of being lady-like, letting out animalistic grunts in time with these new thrusts. I writhed in blissful agony, roiling with the expectation of one massive final climax, building so powerfully within me, it claimed my entire existence in that moment.

I exploded with mind-bending bliss, lost in the crashing waves of a pleasure-storm crashing through me. I nearly lost all sense but had enough awareness to push what I was feeling into my guys. I wanted them to know how they were making me feel... then I wanted them to come... hard.

Falcon cried out and I could almost feel the intensity of his release inside Ceph as Ceph then allowed himself to come and virtually exploded inside me with the heavy throbbing release of a man who'd been on the verge for far too long. And Rhino wasn't far behind, crying out as he pressed deep, his cock pulsing and pounding with the beat of his heart as he surged over and over, filled me. This only served to wring new heights of rapture from me. I was thrown into a warm abyss of unending pleasure; ever so full, ever so loved, ever so needed and fulfilled.

Yup, Leoa purred. *Luckiest woman alive.*

I woke, not realizing I'd passed out.

I was curled up in bed, feeling warm and so *very* satisfied. The guys had cleaned up the bath and brazier and were all in bed with me, pressed close. I snuggled deeper into the three-fold warmth of their embrace and finally — after weeks on the road and all the horrors that had happened before that — allowed myself to fully, truly relax.

CHAPTER 10

LYRAN

Cold winds surged past me and tousled my hair as I rode Eophon high over the vast Maraslad Forest. I had flown ahead of the others to find the new camp Prince Estian had established. The Forest was thick, and it was easy to hide an encampment of that size, except from the air. I'd needed to ensure my group coming from the north, were heading in the right direction.

We'd been travelling through the thick of the forest for weeks, with no roads. The going had been slow. The big Karhukora were not made for these dense thickets, though their hides were tough and they simply lumbered through the undergrowth with little hindering them, which helped to make way for the others. Though it did mean the Njorvasoturi spent most of their evenings plucking branches and leaves off their mounts.

Since no wagons could navigate the undergrowth, Dawn had been moved to a stretcher, carried by Pan and

Swift. She was still insensate, her spirit strong but... distant, her body fading slowly. The three of us were growing more and more worried for her. But... as I'd made this trip, I'd formed a plan that I hoped might break her out of her coma.

I found the others camped less than ten leagues from where I'd left them. I'd been gone for three days, and they hadn't gone far.

There weren't many places where Eophon could easily land, so... we made one. Eophon blasted fire at a portion of the forest — not far from the camp the others were making — incinerating trees. That, of course, started a small forest fire, which Eophon put out as we landed. The inward flap of their giant wings caused the air to be sucked in toward us and the fire came with it, sucked off the growth at the edge of the burned zone until there was nothing but the embers beneath Eophon, which the dragon preferred to sleep upon.

Sleep well, old friend, I said as I tossed myself down from the saddle to the smoldering forest floor.

And you, my friend. I hope your plan works and you can revive your beloved. She is... unique. Even I can feel her spirit. I... like her.

That was high praise indeed. I'd have to let Dawn know... once she was awake again.

I pushed through the forest to the camp, which was massive with the number of people following us. Every night was an ordeal in clearing enough land so these people could sleep. We'd begun crafting hammocks for everyone to simply sling between trees, but only had about three hundred of them, which meant there were more than double that who needed to find some warmth and place to rest.

I found where Pan and Swift had laid Dawn. A tarp had been hung over a rope, creating a crude tent and within many layers of blankets covered the forest floor and upon that make-shift bed rested our beloved.

The other two looked up at me and I could see from the look in their eyes, Dawn's condition hadn't changed. Pan in particular was despondent, verging on panic.

"Good, this will work for what I have planned," I said to them, looking around at the large, safe area they'd created.

"You have a plan?" Pan asked, hope sparking in his amethyst eyes.

I began taking off my armor and the many layers of padding and silks. "Indeed. The plan is simple, if a bit... unorthodox. But since even Astraed the healer doesn't know anything which might work, I figure it's time to try something... a bit outrageous." The two men seemed to agree to this. "I had a lot of time to think on my trip and I hope this will work. You'll probably want to disrobe and, we'll need to get Dawn out of her clothes." That got some raised brows. "The plan is for you two to help her reconnect with her body, and the best way to do that is to... stimulate it, however you wish. I will connect with her spirit and try to seek out her essence and draw her back to her body as well."

"And we need to be naked to do this?" Swift asked, though he shrugged. "Not that I mind. I'm just curious."

"Call it a hunch," I said. "I get the feeling if this works... it may have... repercussions... for all of us." That got a flat look from both men. Perhaps I'd been too vague. "If she wakes up and is highly stimulated, she may wish for us to help her to completion, yes?"

Their eyes lit up and they nodded.

The two of them stripped quickly, then carefully removed Dawn's clothes. By then, I was mostly out of my armor and came to kneel next to dawn's head. Swift and Pan nestled under a heavy blanket with her, their hands caressing her, stroking her, lips kissing softly.

I closed my eyes and found a place of calm within me. I'd never attempted anything like what I was about to do. I'd probably need all my inner strength to do it. Centering myself, I connected with my spirit, feeling its soft and warm pulse within me, like a second heartbeat.

Since my spirit was linked to Eophon's, I felt them here as well.

I will do what I can to aid you, my friend, came the dragon's gruff and rumbling voice within me.

Thank you, Eophon. I suspect I'll need everything I can get.

From this place of spirit, I could already sense Dawn before me. Her spirit was like a beacon and our love had already formed a bond between us, so and I reached out through that. My hope was to merge our essences and delve into her spirit.

It wasn't easy. I had no clue how to do what I was attempting, joining two spirits into one. We were both powerful of spirit and that power didn't want to blend, instead our spirits resisted each other. It felt like we were both bubbles, bouncing off each other, with no true force to make us merge.

So, I stopped pushing and instead tried to simply be next to her spirit. By using force, I'd only pushed her away, but bringing my spirit to hers ever-so-slowly, I managed to get them to touch. Then, like two soap bubbles, we semi-merged into one spirit, but with a boundary, a barrier still between us.

But I knew I was close. The resistance was waning, more ephemeral. I thought of Dawn and all of her amazing qualities: her brash strength and fearless determination. Mostly I focused on my love for her and the connection of our mutually strong spirits. I reached out my arm. I knew my physical limb would have no effect in the place in which I currently dwelled, but the action helped me to push out with just a portion of my spirit, pressing against the gauzy barrier between us. With that focus, that pinpoint of love and connection I pushed upon the barrier and...

I felt a resistance, then...

The wall between us fell and our two spirits became one.

I inhaled deeply as my spirit merged with Dawn's. I was in a place of brightness, a place without form, only... color. My colors were swirling mass of dark blue, mixed with brilliant yellow-gold and flashes of hot white. Every-where around me were hues of conflagration: a swirling mass of burning reds and oranges with flashes of yellow and white. For a moment it was all I could do just to resist the massive force of her spirit. Joined with Eophon, I had thought myself unequaled in spirit. But Dawn and Amya were easily a match for us... which was truly amazing.

I took a long moment to steady myself, acclimatizing to this strange turbulent river of color. Then, from this place, I called out with an internal voice:

Dawn? Can you hear me? Are you there?

Lyran? Is that you? Yet this voice wasn't Dawn's, it had a masculine quality to it. I didn't recognize it.

Who are you? I asked.

I am Amya, Dawn's Lumani. Lyran, is this you? Have you... somehow Bonded with Dawn's spirit?

As much as Dawn had spoken of Amya, her Lumani, I'd not know it had such a strong masculine quality to it. Odd indeed. *Yes. Where is Dawn?*

I don't know. She's here all around us, but... I can't reach her. I can't speak to her. I've been so very worried.

I am hoping I can reach her, perhaps if we did so together, that might help?

I'll try anything. Appearing before me in the flaming spirit of Dawn, was another entity. It had similar colors to Dawn, but the reds were darker, the oranges deeper, the yellows more golden. *Hello Lyran, I am Amya, I have never met another in such a manner as this. It is... intriguing. How would you like to proceed?*

First, can you feel what Swift and Pan are doing? They are trying to stimulate the senses of Dawn's Body.

Oh, yes, I am very aware of their efforts. They are doing a very good job at the moment.

Good. I am hoping part of what will help Dawn return are these pleasant physical sensations.

Ah, a good idea. What's next?

That was the question. If the living spirit within Dawn's own spirit couldn't contact her... how was I going to do so?

Perhaps sensing my uncertainty, Amya tactfully made a suggestion: *Perhaps... since spirit is a place of emotion... I love Dawn dearly, but I do believe your love for her is far greater than mine, yes?*

Yes, in this place it wasn't about voices or thoughts, it was about feelings and my love was certainly a strong connector between us. *You're right, thank you. If you can... add your love to mine, perhaps together we can reach her?*

Our two essences drew close, and tendrils of spirit began to reach out and intertwine between us. I had no true sense of what the colors meant in this place, but I did notice when my golds touched Amya's golds there was a spark of much deeper connection. And if that was the case... then I could reach out with my hot white to Dawn's white and perhaps make a connection as well.

I felt Amya's affection for Dawn, like that of a parent. Though it would be better to say it was like the memory of a parent's affections, living within a person and helping them to grow and strive even after that parent had past. I used that and added it to my own burning love and desire for Dawn as I reached out one of my white tendrils toward the massive storm of colors around me.

And I caught one.

The jolt to my spirit nearly knocked me right out of Dawn. It was like I'd jumped onto the back of a wild stallion, bucking and bouncing and being tossed about by the torrent of its whims. But I held. And through that connection I surged my love in combination with Amya's

Dawn, if you're out there, come to me, please! I whispered into her soul.

And from what seemed like an impossible distance, I heard the faintest of replies.

CHAPTER 11

DAWN

Amidst the nothing in which I floated, I felt a brush of something new, a hint of desire and love, then: *Dawn, if you're out there, come to me, please!* It was Lyran's voice, coming from some great distance, carried on unseen eddies in this vast void.

"Lyran?" I spoke, even though I had no lips. I had no body at all. I was disconnected from everything. I spoke with the memory of speech.

Dawn! Oh, thank the Sacred Fire! Come to me. You need to return to your body!

My body?

But... I was dead.

What else could this place be but death? It was... nothing, devoid of feeling; a lack of everything that was life. I knew I existed, but other than that, I had nothing. This must be death, the eternal void. Certainly, that was one of the theories people had for what happened after we died. I'd never subscribed to any one theory, but I figured I knew now. I had given too much to Astraed to save Lyran and had died.

And now it seemed Lyran was dead too. How else could be reaching me?

"I'm so sorry Lyran. I thought I could save you. Apparently, everything I had, wasn't enough."

What are you talking about Dawn? You did save me, then Pan saved you.

Saved... me?

"But I'm dead. What else could this place be, but the nothingness of death."

No, Dawn... Oh, I see now.

"See what?" Now I was getting confused. I didn't think you could get confused once you were dead. I figured everything would make sense. But I'd been wrong. Even in this void I could still be confused.

You think you're dead, which is why you haven't returned to your body. Oh Dawn, no, you're not dead, your body is alive and waiting for you, but some part of you has been... lost. I was able to connect with your spirit to try to reach you. Please come back to us Dawn, we need you! We... love you.

Come back? That was possible?

I certainly didn't want to be dead... or did I? If I wasn't truly dead, why had I stayed in this place for so long? And I knew the answer as soon as I asked the question: because of the pain. I'd seen Lyran dying and...

For so long now, I'd run from the pain of loss. My parents had been distant, and I'd put up walls around my heart so I wouldn't be hurt like that again. But over the last few months — ever since I'd met Roo and all these wonderful men — the barriers between me and my love had been breaking down. I'd been allowing myself to love... and it had been wonderful. But all this time, some part of me had doubted, had been waiting for someone to leave me.

Then I'd seen Lyran there, wrapped in bandages, barely alive and I'd felt all the pain of another loss surge through me. It had been one reason why I'd asked Astraed to take everything from me; if I couldn't save him, I hadn't been sure I wanted to live with the loss. All my walls had shot up once again, and when I had been drained, I'd come to this place, a place blocked off from feelings, from love. It was safe here.

But having spent so much time here, I knew now... it was empty too. A place without feeling was cold and lonely. Yes, there was no pain, but there was also no warmth, no comfort, no love.

And I *did* have love now. Pan loved me and showed me every day with his dedicated loyalty. Swift loved me, I saw it in how his eyes grew large and he gave that warm grin every time he looked at me. And Lyran... he'd come into my very soul to find me. I felt his love through how much he respected me, seeing me as an equal despite having a dragon at his command. And I didn't want to distance myself from any of that anymore. Yes, there was suffering and pain in life, but there was also pleasure, warmth, and... love.

And I wanted my loves back... now!

Which meant leaving this cold, dark void. I pushed myself toward Lyran's voice, his essence. I felt the void shift. The nothingness began to give way to swirling light, my light, my spirit, I recognized it instantly. And as I pulled myself to Lyran, I saw him and Amya. I knew them even without physical form. Amya with his dark-reds and golden hues. Lyran, with that indigo — the same as his eyes — swirling with gold and white.

I'm here! I said, excited to finally be out from that nothingness. And as soon as I made that proclamation... I felt... so much more than my spirit. I could feel my body, distant, but definitely there, and... being very well loved at the moment. *Ohhhhhh!*

Dawn! Can you feel yourself?

Oh... yes, yes, very much.

Swift and Pan are... stimulating you, in hopes of you returning to your body.

And you... I said to Lyran. *I can feel you, your spirit. We're connected.* And I saw the burning white tendrils of my spirit mingling with the same color in his. And through that I felt the true intensity of his affection and desire, the full depths of his love for me.

Even without my body, that was enough to make my spirit fill with so much bliss I knew my body was reacting.

And... I wanted more.

Without knowing how, I reached past Lyran, past my own barriers to find the spirits of those around me.

A whole new world opened up. Perhaps this was

some new level of my spirit-gift, I didn't know, but suddenly I felt the spirits of all life around me, from the massive forms of the Karhukora, to the tiniest insects. The world was alive with life... and close by, I felt Pan and Swift. I knew them, even though all I saw were the colors of their spirits. Pan was nearly all a blinding white, with thin tendrils of many other colors, the most predominant were dark purples and deep violets. And within Pan was Eona: so earthy, deep blues and greens in shimmering shades, swirling together. Swift was an intriguing mix of gleaming silvers — with threads of the hot white we all seemed to share — and many shades of blue, green, and red. And within Swift was Isoa, shimmering white and gold. Oddly, I sensed another spirit — twin to Swift's — attached to his. I could even see it, though through some haze, and I knew it was Falcon, distant as his body was.

I reached out to Pan and Swift, my white to their white, and connected with them. I pulled them into me, and I felt the thrust of their love and yearning for me.

Oh! Lyran breathed.

Yes, I said, burning and bubbling with the force of my lovers' spirits inside me.

Lyran? Dawn? Dawn! Swift was ecstatic.

Dawn! I love you! Pan said the words, but I also felt the pure force of emotion from him, a wave of warm devotion.

We all love you, Lyran said softly, and I felt his spirit caressing mine.

The four of us were merged into one. The extremity

of their need for me, and mine for them... overwhelmed us, smashing into each of us like a tidal wave and carrying us along.

Bodies may sometimes take time to arouse to bliss, but emotions can spark instantly to great passion, and that is exactly what we did. My longing to be with them after so long joined with the intensity of their desire for me and we exploded into heated euphoria.

I was in the throes of an ecstasy unlike any I'd felt before, the full and complete arousal of my soul, my entire being. And... I was sharing that with not only my guys... but all of their Bonded as well. And with the combined power of all of our spirits swelling to incredible heights of passion and fervor, we were having, what was — and probably would be — our most powerful orgasmic event ever. Distantly, I knew my body was writhing with a series of orgasms, and I relished in the knowing that all my guys were having the same. During my first time, with the pleasure-workers in Weijin, I'd learned that men generally could not have orgasm after orgasm in quick succession, but women could. Well, my men were feeling what that was like now, what they often gave me. They were brought again and again to the highest of pleasure, mounting and building and releasing over and over. And I sensed how that was blowing their minds.

And giddy with release and power — knowing it would make a horrible mess in the real world — I shunted us all back into our bodies.

My eyes snapped open as my body tensed so hard only my head and heels were touching the ground. The power of a spiritual orgasm filled me, and I cried out as my body contracted over and over in a series of releases so violent, I felt it in my fingers and toes, and... I was making a rather large wet spot on the blankets around me. But I didn't really care as the pure pleasure was unlike anything I'd ever felt before. The rawest condensation of bliss.

And around me, I heard the guys grunting and groaning. I felt the bodies of those closest to me twitching and quivering.

It lasted for some time, washing through us in waves, each ever-so-slightly less powerful than the last until I was so giddy I was actually laughing as my body finally began to relax. Even then I was still experiencing minor orgasms, more sedate and soothing, filling me with tingling joy.

"What in the Sacred Fires was that?" Lyran said, his voice tremulous and gasping. "Oh, Dragon's Teeth, I... I'm sorry Dawn."

Sorry? For what?

I rolled my head to the side. He knelt close, not far from my head. His cock was still semi-aroused, twitching as it slowly came to rest... but he'd made quite the mess: on the blankets, on himself... on me.

I just laughed. It was my fault for returning us to our bodies. I hadn't known he was kneeling next to my head.

Swift and Pan, to either side of me, began chuckling as well.

"We're going to want to burn these blankets I think," Swift said and after that none of us could stop laughing. We were so full of joy and the sweet stupor of our elation.

Lyran was the least messy of us. He used a still dry edge of a blanket to clean himself, then went to get us water and cloth for bathing.

That was sexy and stimulating as well, as we washed each other. I was just happy to be back, to feel my body and all the wonderful sensations my guys could produce. And they were happy to have me back and showed me all their love and affection.

Once we were clean and new blankets had been procured, we all huddled together, warm and content.

It was only then... that I realized something and began laughing once again.

"What?" Swift asked.

All I could say was: "I'm fairly certain Falcon felt that too. I hope he wasn't doing anything important."

CHAPTER 12

RHINO

It was quite late when Falcon groaned so loud it woke me. Then he began swearing. He rose from the bed but seemed unable to walk. By then, we were all awake.

"Falcon what's wrong?" Roo asked.

"Nothing!" he grunt-shouted, leaning heavily on the wall. He made it perhaps halfway to the privy before he let out the most intense yell of a groan and proceeded to have a rather prolonged release right there.

We were all taken just a little aback by this.

It was Ceph who spoke first, whispering to Roo. "Apparently sex with you is so potent that hours later, his dreams make him come."

She blinked at that, surprised, though we couldn't deny what was happening before us. We probably shouldn't have watched, but it was just a little engrossing. And when Falcon finally collapsed to his knees and began a soft giddy laugh, the rest of us finally moved and went to him.

"Are you... well?" Roo asked.

"Oh yes... very much so," he said through his bliss-intoxicated laugh. "Something... very powerful just happened to Swift... and I experienced it as well."

Roo was playfully scandalized when she said: "So that wasn't for me?"

Falcon was now partially crying he was laughing so hard. "I really don't know what that was. All I know is, I have a mess to clean up."

Ceph nodded and made to return to bed with a muttered comment: "Wish I was connected to his brother too."

We all laughed at that.

Soon enough, Falcon had wiped down the wall and floor and himself and returned to bed with us.

But I didn't sleep well after that, and it seemed far too soon that the sky outside our many windows began to lighten.

We all rose, washed, and dressed. When we left, a servant outside our room nodded to us and told us to follow her. We were taken to a dining hall, and the servant indicated a table where Commander Lucjan was breaking her fast with a few others in uniform and armor.

I'd been working on controlling my presence around others, with Iomu giving me the benefit of her knowledge. Yet, I hadn't had many situations to put it into practice. I did so now: moderating my body-language, shoulders slouched, head tilted forward. I kept as still as possible, my movements small, and I made sure to smile a lot. I didn't know if it was working, or if the others at the table were just used to being respected and showed deference, but they didn't seem intimidated by my size.

Lucjan nodded to us as we joined them. As we were brought food — minimal as it was — the commander introduced us to the others at the table. "Lady Roo and Lords Falcon, Rhino, and Ceph, it is my pleasure to introduce my brother, King Frydryk, my uncle Lord-General Makar, and his daughter, my cousin, Captain Myra." The three were a study in contrasts. The king was of indeterminate age, probably late twenties or early thirties, thin and tall with blond hair and intense blue eyes. Compared to Lucjan, his sister, he seemed small and slight. Lord Makar was a husky man with more grey than black in his hair and bushy beard, with a hard look about him. Captain Myra was of square and sturdy build, like her father, but smaller and compact, with a cocky grin and dancing golden eyes under her messy mop of dark hair. "We're all that remains of the royal line of Osera." At that, the king's expression grew dark and grim. He seemed ashamed, bitter. An odd expression for one who ruled this nation.

Roo reached out to the king, taking his hand. "I'm so sorry for your loss," she said softly.

He blinked at her, then shot a look at his sister. Lucjan shook her head. "I told them nothing."

"How did you know of my wife?" the king said, suspicious, accusing.

Roo sighed. "I didn't. But I can... sense people's emotions. And I sensed from you a keen and close sense of loss. I knew only that you'd lost someone and it still seemed fresh to you."

"It was four years ago," Lucjan said softly.

Oh...?

Myra piped up. "The queen was a brave woman. She died stopping the assassins who'd been sent to kill the king."

That could explain the shame the king seemed to be feeling, and the bitterness: if he hadn't been able to defend himself and his wife had had to save him?

"And with her went her unborn child, the future of Osera," Lucjan finished.

"Who are these strangers to whom you so freely spill our secrets?" the king demanded. But he didn't wait for an answer. "I don't care what you say, I don't trust them and we should tell them no more!" He rose sharply, face red with fury, and I assumed still a heavy dose of shame and self-loathing. "But I obviously don't have a say in my own country anymore!" He turned and left in a huff.

The tension at the table quickly vanished as the other three sighed. "Four years and he hasn't changed," Makar said softly.

"I still don't see why Lucjan can't be king... or queen, whatever. She's the one running things anyway," Myra said, then raised her hands in surrender as the other two both glared at her.

Lucjan sighed. "My brother probably would have made a fine king... in peaceful times." She sighed. "But he was made king the year the Thraian's arrived, when my father and what little army we'd had, tried to stand against the invasion. I was the one who'd studied warfare, while Frydryk studied diplomacy and etiquette. I was to take over the armies from my uncle when he passed."

"Not happening any time soon, lass," Makar said with a chuckle.

"I know. Trust me, I am happy you are still with us."

"You'd do fine on your own... better than your brother." Makar then seemed to catch himself and shook his head. It was clear these three didn't think much of the king but had to keep themselves from demeaning him to the general public. Makar turned to us. "I hear you're going to get rid of the Thraian boats? How exactly do you plan on doing that?"

Ceph answered before I could, which was good, because I had no clue what the plan was. "Simple." Ceph didn't seem concerned. "We'll sneak in tonight and burn their boats and their boat building facilities. Falcon will fly us in and drop and us off. We'll steal some oil from their camp, toss it on the boats, light a spark, and flee."

"Just like that?"

"I said simple, not easy."

Makar huffed a laugh. "Indeed." An odd looked pass

over his face and he looked at Lucjan. "How many boats would we need to get all the civilians off the island?"

She raised a brow. "All at once? Well over a hundred, assuming they were the standard dory, and that's assuming we packed them full."

Makar grimaced.

"What are you thinking?" I asked. "You want us to steal boats instead of burning them?"

Makar nodded slowly. "With food becoming a scarce resource, and depending on how well the war goes, we may want to get those who can't fight off the island. It's something we've been thinking of for some time, but they wouldn't have anywhere to go. The only place we could send them is the north-east shore of the lake, and there isn't anywhere to go from there, until we learned of your rebels that was. Do you think your camp could support a thousand more people?"

That was a lot.

None of us answered quickly. It was Roo who finally spoke up. "If you wish to get these people away, we will do everything we can to ensure they are safe. Certainly, food will be more readily available on the shore, if you have some hunters in the group."

Makar nodded. "We have seven boats in our own protected harbor. We use them for night fishing or getting supplies from those on the far shore. If we were to try to use them to ferry people to the far shore, it would take over twenty trips. And I don't think we can steal a hundred boats, but perhaps... eighteen or twenty? With that many we could ferry the civilians to shore in five or six trips. That's doable in a single night." He looked at me and Ceph. "You think you could steal that many boats?"

"Not on our own," Ceph said. If you had a few trusted people — good swimmers — you could send with us, perhaps eight to twelve? Then it might be doable."

Makar nodded. "That is possible. How would that change your plans?"

"Significantly," Ceph said. "Rhino and I would go in and have to quietly clean the docks of guards, so your men could take the time to tie a few boats together, then get away. And they won't be moving quickly when they leave, so Rhino and I will have to provide a distraction. We'd start the fire then, burn what we can. And we'd be the last ones out." Ceph shook his head. "It wouldn't be easy at all. Just destroying the boats is one thing, but needing to stay and guard the backs of others while they steal them, that's..." His expression was grim.

Suicide. We were all thinking it.

I don't know, I think it could be fun! Iomu said with her usual manic excitement.

You always want me to run into danger.

There was a reason I chose a big, strapping man like you to Bond with. I knew you could take it. I've been waiting for you to come along for three lifetimes, you're tough and strong and big and amazing. You can do anything. Together, we can do anything! She was always like this, into extremes and wild abandon. I usually had to keep her in check. But... she'd also saved my life a few times. She was an experienced warrior had helped me survive back when I'd been poorly trained. Since then, I'd learned a lot. Though, I didn't particularly want to be standing on the end of a dock fighting thousands of Thraians.

Why not? You can take them!

I didn't respond.

"Will you do it?" Makar asked, since Ceph's response hadn't been conclusive. The lord-general looked at me and Ceph.

We looked at each other. I... nodded slowly.

Ceph sighed and nodded. "We'll do it."

And that's how I found myself — that night — dropped onto the enemy docks. The Oserans had found me some armor, amazingly there were pieces that actually fit me. I had a long chain shirt under a breastplate, pauldrons, grieves and bracers... and I had a massive sword, which somehow felt natural in my hands, certainly it was the only weapon I'd ever held that seemed the right size for me.

Ceph was next to me, in simple black leather armor — and draped in black to blend in with the night — with two long swords and a grim look in his eyes, the only part of him I could see.

We crouched behind a large supply box at the end of one pier. The full enemy camp was perhaps a mile inland behind us, but there were still many Thraians out here guarding the docks and their boat-building facilities.

We waited amongst the shadows. The occasional

Thraian guard would come out and lean on the large box we were hiding behind, but never came around it.

Then, with barely any sound I could discern, a man climbed up the end of the dock, hands and head appearing close to our feet. He was drenched — having swum here — and dressed all black. Armor would have been useful for their return trip but would have tired them out on the swim here. He nodded to us.

The Oserans had arrived. It was time to go to work.

I veered into my avatar and began flying down the docks. I'd trained all day with Ceph at something he called 'hit and fade,' where I flew in as a beetle, transformed attacked, then veered again before the enemy could attack. Ceph himself needed to be stealthy and careful, I could be a bit more reckless, as long as I veered in time and people didn't know to target the beetle.

You'll do well, this is amazing. I'm so excited. Let's slaughter these bastards! Iomu was getting a bit too worked up.

I found two guards at the base of the pier.

I flew in behind them. One of them must have heard my buzzing wings and turned.

I transformed and slashed at him with my large sword. It was far too easy to cleave through him. This was my first time using such a heavy weapon in my powerful hands... and knowing how to use it. It seemed like there should have been more resistance when cutting through a body, but apparently not for one with my strength. I was a but stunned.

It's 'cause you're so strong! Now kill the other one, quick! Don't just stand there!

I slashed up at the second guard and he let out a clipped cry as he died. Then I was back in beetle form.

Unfortunately, that bit of noise the second guard had made had alerted others. They found the bodies quickly and raised alarm even as I flashed in among that group of three and cut them down. I couldn't stop them from alerting others, and now the alarm was spreading quickly.

We'll just have to kill them all then! Iomu said cheerfully. She was one bloodthirsty Lumani.

I had a plan though. I made a line directly inland, killing a few men here and there, making it obvious where I'd been. I left a clear trail of dead men behind me. I wanted to draw attention away from the docks and make it seem like I was heading for their main camp. So, I kept popping in, killing one or two men, then popping out, heading deeper and deeper into enemy territory. Soon, the word seemed to get around that there was some invisible and powerful threat heading for the main camp. More and more men gathered, and it was getting harder to find to a smaller group to attack.

I popped in behind a large group and cut down two men with one stroke, but others had noticed and even as I veered back, lamplight caught me, people saw me.

"It's that beetle!"

"It's a man!"

"The man turned into a beetle."

"Kill it!"

And then things got really interesting. The night was alive with zinging crossbow bolts and arrows trying to hit me, it was everything I could do, just to fly erratically and evade them. I flew higher and higher into the darkness of the night, and eventually the missiles stopped. I began to make my way back to the docks, hoping the Thraians would think I was heading inland, since that's what I'd done so far.

It seemed most of them did, but when I got to the docks, things were not going well.

A few of the Oseran men were down, being helped into boats by others. That would mean they'd not be able to steal as many boats as they'd hoped.

Ceph was fighting for his life and was a blur of movement, far deadlier and more devastating than I felt I'd ever be.

He's got half a decade of training on you. You'll get there. But also, experience is the best teacher, now get down there and help him!

Iomu was right.

I landed nearby and returned to myself, cutting down two men who'd been heading for Ceph before they fully registered I was there.

"Thank the Spirits! There you are! Where have you been?"

"Luring people inland."

"Oh... makes sense. I was wondering why there weren't more guards out here. Still!" His tone was harsh, and he said all this while the man fought of three guards at once.

I joined the fight, not getting too close to Ceph, but guarding his back as much as I could.

"How many boats?" I asked.

"I think we got eighteen, but I'm not sure."

The last Oserans were just pushing off from the docks now, they had four boats tied in a line behind them, struggling to paddle away. We needed to give them more time.

But the two of us would soon be overwhelmed.

I slashed through three men with one long stroke, then planted my sword in the wood beneath us and began picking up bodies. Between the two of us, we'd killed a lot of men, and I surged my strength, throwing the dead at our feet at the new men who were arriving. They screamed at the horrific onslaught, some jumping off the dock entirely.

To add to what I hoped was a frightening affect, I roared as loud as I could into the night.

"Blessed Spirits!" Ceph hissed. "That was terrifying; you're terrifying!"

"That's the point! Now get out of here!" Then I plucked up my sword, roared again, and charged the mass of men heading for us.

They balked and halted, some ran, but a few didn't. The first crossbow bolt passed so close to my head that I heard the high-pitched whine as it nicked my ear, which stung, but didn't stop me. The next one hit my side, taking a chunk out of my love-handles. That didn't stop me.

I reached them and began cutting them down. I roared, while Iomu sang madly in my head.

Then a bolt took me full in my left thigh, hard and deep and instantly knocked me off my feet.

The enemy were all over me. Fists pummeled, blades slashed and pierced. I roared again, flailing wildly with arms and legs. I'd lost my sword, but my fists were devastating, and I knew I'd sent several men flying with one punch, but I felt more and more blood leaking out of me. I was going cold, growing weak.

Then suddenly... everything went dark... and wet... and sticky.

Then... just dark.

CHAPTER 13

DAWN

"BLOODY BASTARD! CURSE HIM TO THE DEEPEST DEPTHS OF The Blackest Pits!" I needed to hit something or scream. Screaming would be less painful, so I let out a long bellow of rage.

"Dawn, calm down, he only left yesterday, perhaps we can catch him and stop him." Lyran was levelheaded. I expected him to be angrier at Prince Estian, but he wasn't.

The Basian prince had gotten the refugees and the small rebel force to an excellent spot in the Maraslad forest, perhaps two days north of the Basian border. Then, just before we'd gotten back, he'd decided to take some of our forces and raid a northern Basian outpost.

But the man couldn't raid a pantry, let alone a fortified outpost. He was going to get himself — and our forces — killed! And we needed him if we were going to restore the crown to Basia once this fighting was all over.

I'd been looking forward to settling down in one place for a bit after months of travelling, but that was not to be.

Calm yourself, Amya said stoically. *Running off in a rage will only compound the error, you need to think rationally.*

She was right. I drew in a long breath and tried to find some peace. "You're right. Let's go, if we take Eophon we can—"

"No, I won't risk Eophon being seen. The Thraians would know we'd moved north; that *I'd* moved north. Right now, even if they catch Prince Estian, they don't necessarily know he's with me. I don't think they much fear him or any rabble he could muster to resist them. But me... they'd come after me with everything they have."

I didn't have much faith in the man though. "Yes, but if he's caught, he'll tell them everything. They'll know you're here soon enough."

Lyran nodded. "I know, but still, we'll hurry as best we can on horseback, even though the forest will slow us considerably. That will have to do."

Already he was readying a horse, as was Pan. Actually, Pan was readying two, one for me as well. Swift was already out scouting to see if he could find the wayward prince.

So, we left the northerners in the care of one of Lyran's lieutenants to get themselves settled at the camp. Then we rode as fast as we could that day, though the forest restricted our pace, as we'd anticipated.

Swift found us that evening, reporting that we weren't

far from where the forest thinned out, then gave way to rolling hills. Farther out was a rushing river, which was the northern border of Basia, or so he guessed. The outpost and a small village were just on the other side of that river. He estimated another day and a half of travel at least, and that was with hard riding once we were out in the open. He also reported no sight of the Basian prince.

We quickly discussed it and decided to move on through the night. Pan and I had excellent night vision to help guide us through the forest.

Sometime after midnight, the forest began to thin out and we mounted for some light riding. Once the sun was up, Swift led us. We'd all been travelling non-stop for months and after one night without rest, we were fatigued. Swift, however, had inherited an ability from his avatar to go without sleep. Apparently, swifts could put half their brain to sleep at a time, maintaining low function of the body. Essentially, he could walk and remain somewhat alert while part of his brain was asleep.

We did stop, just before midday, for a quick rest. Lyran's connection to his dragon meant he also needed less sleep. I too was feeling well enough after the short rest, but Pan was looking weary still. Fey were usually hardy and didn't need as much sleep as humans, but I suspected he was still soul-weary from all that time worrying about me, when I'd been unconscious.

We rode hard, resting ourselves and the horses when needed, and by the end of that day we came to the river. We were all near to fall-down exhausted as we lay on a hill overlooking the river and the outpost. The sky to the west was still vaguely lit, but full night had fallen over us. Torches, lanterns, and fires from the village and the outpost gave us some sense for the layout. The outpost was a basic motte and bailey design, with a tower at the top of a hill and a basic wooden palisade around the yard.

Prince Estian had taken fifty of our men on this raid, a quarter of Lyran's initial rebel force. There was no sign of them anywhere. We should have caught up to them if they hadn't attacked yet. That meant it was likely they had tried to raid the fort... and been completely ineffectual.

My anger at the prince was growing with every fatigued breath I took. How could he have been so stupid! *Bloody stupid prick!*

You've had your fair share of brash acts, Amya reminded me.

There is a vast difference between brash and stupid. I may be impulsive and take radial action, but I still know enough not to overreach my own abilities. I do think things through, even if they are... extreme things.

"It shouldn't be too hard to sneak into that outpost," Swift said. "Dawn and I could get in easily to take a look around."

"That is probably the best plan. Just... stay in your avatar forms as much as possible," he grumbled. It was clear he wanted to go with us.

We nodded and veered. Swift plucked me up and flew low over the river before surging up to the top of the hill on which the tower was situated. There, at the base of the tower, he set me down and landed next to me. His avatar form wasn't as large or strong as his brother's and just carrying my little kangaroo-rat was a lot for him. He quickly transformed, whispering: "Take a look around the base of the tower and through the bailey, see what you can see. I'll try higher up in the tower, and we'll meet back here when we're done." I had no way to respond to him, but I bobbed my body in a semblance of a nod. He nodded, veered, and took off.

I scurried around the base of the square tower, finding no easy way in, even for a little thing like me. It was a solidly build structure. I could take some time to chew through some wood or burrow a bit, but I didn't have the luxury of time. So, I ran down the hill to the bailey to look around. But before I got to the low buildings of the bailey, I heard something. My kangaroo-rat form had very keen hearing and something at the base of the hill had caught my ears. I ran around the base of the hill and came to, what looked like, cellar doors, roughly laid into the hillside. I was able to scurry under the doors and found steps leading down. It was dark in here, but I got the sense of a mine-like shaft, girded with wood, descending into the earth.

Now that I was on the other side of the doors, the sound I'd heard earlier was clearer and I was sure of it now: people groaning, in pain.

I wasn't sure I wanted to know what was down here, but still I ran down the steps as fast as I could and began to see light up ahead. Then the light resolved into a cave-like room. It had walls of stone, but not natural. This was fieldstone, which had been fitted to make strong walls to hold up the wooden beams of the ceiling, keeping the earth above us from falling in.

Cages lined either side of a narrow hall running through the center of the room to what looked like a smaller room on the far side.

Three guards sat on chairs or walked the hall. In the cages were wounded men. I didn't know Lyran's men by sight, but they were still wearing some of the rag-tag armor and tabards they had when they'd ambushed Roo and I on the road. These were at least some of the men Estian had brought on his raid, but there looked to be only a dozen or so. Where were the other forty? Dead? My rage at Estian boiled over.

Perhaps it was my anger that made me act a bit rashly in that moment.

Dawn, you're not thinking of...

I ignored Amya and acted.

Flashing back to my human form, I had my sword out and had slashed one of the guard's throats before he knew what was happening.

Two steps and I was at another. He had his sword half out of his scabbard as he died.

The guard patrolling the hall between the cages, was running toward me, weapon out. I spun out of the way of his long slash, dropping and kicking out with one leg to sweep his legs out from under him. I came up smoothly as he collapsed, and he was dead a moment later.

I found the keys and went to the cells.

"Who are you?" someone asked.

"That's the princess, the one we ambushed on the road," another said.

"Exactly," I whispered. "Where are the rest of the men?"

"Dead or lost."

I ground my teeth. These ones looked rough enough. Half of them could walk well enough, looking tired and wounded. The rest needed to be helped to move at all. We'd not be getting anywhere quickly with this lot.

One of them told the story as we slowly made our way back to the stairs. "Prince Estian was desperate for a fight. We got to the river mid-morning and our sergeant suggested we wait for dark, but the prince forced us across that river in broad daylight. It's got some current to it and nearly half our men were washed downstream somewhere. I hope they made it back to camp. The rest of us followed him as he tried to take the keep, climbing the wall and yelling like a madman as he waved his sword around, barely hitting anything. We were quickly overwhelmed, and the prince was captured. Those of us remaining surrendered. The prince was taken up to the keep. He may still be there. I don't even think we've been in here a full day."

So, the attack had been that morning.

"Get these men up the stairs and hopefully one of

these keys unlocks the door at the top." I tossed the key ring to one of the healthier men. "I'm going to see if I can arrange a way out for you." I ran up the stairs in human form, that was quicker, then slipped out under the door in my avatar form. From there, I ran across the yard to what looked like the stables.

I peeked inside and saw a small area near the door with tools, including what I was looking for: rope. I looked around for a stable-hand or a guard. I could hear grunting nearby but couldn't see anything. Curious I ran inside the stables and peeked into the first stall. I found it empty of horses but not unoccupied. A guard had the stable boy bent over and both seemed to be enjoying themselves.

I ran over to the tools, transformed, stole the rope, then crept carefully — no longer in my sneaky avatar form — back to the hill-side cellar doors. The soldiers were just coming out when I got there.

"Take this, get over the wall." I looked around. There was a dark spot along the wall toward the back side of the hill. "There. Hopefully, no lookouts will see you. Wait by the river for myself and my comrade. Hopefully we'll join you with the prince soon." The men nodded, took the rope and made for where the tall tower shadowed the wall from the moon's light.

I transformed and ran back up the hill. Swift was waiting for me. I hoped he had good news. We both transformed in the shadow of the tower.

"The prince isn't here," he said quickly. "He was here,

I saw his fancy armor, but unless there is some underground prison, he's not in the tower."

"There is an underground prison," I said, disappointed at this news. "I found some of the men who came on the raid and got them out." I sighed. "But the prince wasn't with them. We need more info. Is there someone important-looking up there, sleeping?"

Swift grinned. "Yup. Shall I take you to him?"

I nodded.

We both veered and I was quickly carried up to a window. It was narrow, little more than an arrow slit, but we could both squeeze through in our avatar forms. Inside was a dark room, which seemed to take up most of this floor of the tower. The room was sparce, but did have a large bed, and asleep in that bed was a man.

We shifted back to normal, and I whispered, "Get on top of him, make sure he can't go anywhere." Swift nodded and the two of us acted together. He leapt on top of the man pinning him beneath the sheets, while I clamped a hand over his mouth and put a sword to his throat.

The man woke, surprised and trying to cry out, but I stifled it well enough. In the dark I could see the man's panicked eyes, moving between the two of us.

I kept my voice low and lethal. "You have two choices," I said. "Either you tell us what we want to know in a nice soft voice, and you remain alive. Or your cry out as soon as I remove my hand you die. Do you want to die?"

The man gave a shake of his head.

"You'll cooperate?"

A nod.

I removed my hand, but not my sword. "You captured a man in fancy armor today. What did you do with him?"

"The prince?" the man said softly. "We sent him south to Surrin Town."

I would have asked how he knew the man was a prince, but I guessed Estian had been very vocal about who he was and that he should be treated with respect, and so on.

"What's in Surrin Town?" I asked.

"The Thraian Dragon Lord."

Pits!

Well things had just gotten a lot more complicated.

"How far away is Surrin Town?" Could we ride hard and try to catch the prince before he got there?"

"It's about a day's ride. But the carriage would be going through the night. They'll be there by mid-morning tomorrow."

Blackened, Bloody Bones in The Deepest, Darkest Pits! We'd not be able to catch them.

"Thank you, kindly," I said. "I said I'd keep you alive and I will. We're going to go now, and you're not going to make a peep until you've counted to..." I needed a high number this man might actually be able to count to. "...count to twenty, twenty times. Got it?"

The man nodded.

I turned to Swift. "Stay with him till he's half done, then follow me."

Swift nodded. He'd just be able to fly away easily enough.

I went to the narrow window, veered, scurried through, then transformed back as I fell. With the jumping capabilities of my avatar, I'd be able to land this fifty-foot fall easily enough. I landed, sprinted to the wall where the last of the men were just getting over. I leapt and easily cleared the wall, landing on the banks of the river on the other side.

Several of the men gasped, but luckily none cried out.

Now came the hard part... trying to get these men back across the river — at night no less — without losing any more of them.

You think you could jump across? Amya asked.

The river was about fifty feet wide, but I guessed it was deep enough to wash away fully grown men in its swift current.

Probably. Let's give it a go.

I was stronger than I looked and gently picked up one of the wounded men.

"Try not to cry out," I whispered to him, then leaped. It was close, with the added weight of the man, but I landed lightly on the other side. I set the man down and repeated the process.

Swift joined me when I was half done.

Oddly, the man in the tower never called out at all, which meant we got the rest of the men across the river safely and back to Lyran. He was happy to see some of his men had survived.

I told Pan and Lyran about the prince.

Lyran swore.

"What do we do?" I asked.

"No choice," Lyran said. "We can't let my brother interrogate him or our camp is done for. We need to go after him."

As I'd suspected.

The prince had put us in an impossible situation, and we'd have to go into the jaws of the dragon to get him out.

CHAPTER 14

ROO

"WE'LL TAKE CARE OF THEM. I'LL MAKE SURE THE Thraians don't harm a single one of them," I said to Lucjan. We were in the 'war room' up in the tower — where we'd first met the commander — and I was outlining my plan to help the civilians of Osera escape to Lyran's encampment.

"You can do that? Just... poof... get rid of the Thraians? Why don't you just do that then?"

I laughed. "It's not 'just poof' and I can't do it until I'm closer to them, and it won't kill them, just... put them to sleep." I was fairly certain if I pushed extreme calm, peace, and relaxation into anyone on the far shore, especially in the middle of the night when this was going to happen, they'd just fall asleep. Either that or they wouldn't really care to fight or follow us. I'd never tried this on a large area or a significant amount of people before, but I believed I could do it.

"Oh." I could see the skepticism and awe in the commander's eyes.

"I can meddle with people's emotions," I said by way of explanation. "I can incite them to fury." I pushed a little bit of righteous anger into the commander. "Or I can calm them to a light sleep state." I then calmed her right down.

She blinked. "You were... on me... Oh... yes, I do feel a bit drowsy. Can you perk me up again?"

I kept her at peace but added in a bit of stalwart determination.

"Ah... yes, thank you. Wow." She looked at me. "That is... amazing."

I beamed. "I'm just glad we can help."

"And this will be a great help, thank you. I do not know how the war will go, but we will not give up our island easily and not having to worry about those who cannot fight will be a great boon."

"How soon will they be ready to leave?" I asked.

The commander smiled. "We're well organized here. They'll be ready to leave tonight."

"Then so shall we," I said. We'd only been there for a couple of days and though Falcon had been doing this best — exhausted at the end of every day — to get food to the island, it hadn't been much. I was hesitant to ask, but I feared for these people. "How... long do you think you'll be able to hold out... once you're cut off from the mainland entirely?"

Lucjan gave a sad smile. "Militarily, with the men we

have, we can hold these walls indefinitely until the Thraians build a lot more boats or get other help." She sighed. "But yes, food will start to become very scarce. And if the empire figures out they can pick off our night fishermen, we'd have nearly no food. I estimate we have three months of supplies, we could probably go as long as six months, but that would be extremely stretching it."

I nodded, solemnly. "I'll see what I can do about sending along some aid, once I'm back at camp. I... don't know if I'll be able to, but I'll try."

The commanded nodded. "Thank you. You've done so much for us already." She drew in a long breath and drew herself up. "We'll hold, as long as we can."

I admired her bravery and courage. "I know you will."

We parted and I went to make preparations for that evening.

She is a brave woman and loves her people. But all it would take is one dragon lord and this island would be destroyed. Leoa's tone was sad and a bit hard. *She should just come with us!*

This is her home? Would you abandon The Mists so easily?

No... but still.

It is her choice.

It's the wrong one.

I sighed.

In our room I found Rhino awake, finally. He'd been resting, unconscious since the boat raid.

"What happened?" he asked sitting up slowly. He

seemed week, sore. I didn't blame him, even after Ceph had healed him, he'd looked a mess.

"You nearly died, and would have, if I hadn't saved you," Ceph said, coming to sit on the edge of the bed. "I squirted some ink at those attacking you and managed to drag you away from them to a place where we could hide for a moment. Then I healed you... well as best as I couldn't without killing myself. You were... very injured. Then—" Ceph's voice was rising with every sentence. He'd been rather angry with Rhino when he'd returned. It seemed he hadn't fully gotten over that yet. "—I swam with your heavy ass through however many miles of lake to get you back here."

"Oh," Rhino said, suitably abashed. "Sorry."

Ceph sighed and smiled, his voice changed to a soft and sympathetic tone. He laid a hand on Rhino's shoulder. "I'm just glad you survived." Then he was instantly back to harsh and accusing, with a slight slap on that same shoulder. "But don't do anything that stupid again!"

Rhino nodded. "I won't." Then he gave a bark of a laugh. "Actually, I probably will. You don't know what it's like living with Iomu, she's... relentless. I think it's just who I am, or who I'm becoming anyway: I run toward danger not away."

"Bloody big oaf." Ceph shook his head.

"Yeah," Rhino agreed with a nod.

Then we began our preparations for that night.

For most of the rest of the day, the guys helped out with getting the boats and people ready. We'd be sending nine-hundred-and-seventy-three people to shore. We had twenty-three boats, which could hold eight to ten people. We should be able to get everyone across in five trips, but I left that planning to them. Given what I would have to do that night... I rested.

But night came soon enough.

We said our goodbyes to Lucjan, Lord General Makar, and Captain Myra. The king didn't see us off. Then the water-gates were opened, and the boats were loaded and sent out. I was on the first.

The night was dark, clouds covered the moon. Fisherman, who had learned to paddle quietly, barely disturbing the water, rowed us toward the north-east shore. It was eerily quiet, save for the soft, rhythmic swish of the oars.

The sound reminded me of calm days on the ocean as a girl and young woman. But these were not calm days, and I had a task to do.

Lend me any strength you can, I asked Leoa

Everything I have is yours.

I closed my eyes — kneeling, low and steady in the prow of the boat — and reached out my emotional sense toward the far shore. I reached out as far as I could, sensing myriad beings — many of which I assumed were animals from their more primal emotions — along the shore in either direction, then inland as well.

My head began to ache. Sweat beaded on my forehead and pooled between my breasts from the effort of seeking farther and farther afield. Finally, I was certain that anyone or anything out there — beyond my range — wouldn't know these people would be coming ashore. They'd be too far away to see or hear anything. Then... I began to pull at their emotions. It would take too long, too much effort to distinguish between man and beast, so I simply pulled at them all. I took their fear, their curiosity, their lust, their apprehension and more, and I replaced it with peace, and tranquility, with stillness and the serenity of a relaxed soul. I could feel the various beings come to rest, to a placid neutrality. Then... as I'd hoped, I began to sense a shift in their emotional state, which I didn't recognize at first but came to believe was various beings falling asleep.

I was leaning heavily on the gunnels of the boat, drenched in sweat by the time I was finished, and that was roughly when my boat reached the far shore.

The nearly two hundred people disembarked from their many boats about as quietly as might be expected with so many people. They tried their best to keep quiet, but there were splashes and gasps at the coldness of the water. Then... we were all ashore and the boats were rowing back. They would need to repeat that trip four more times. And while they did... the rest of us waited.

Ceph slipped into the shadows to scout. Falcon also flew out to see if he could see any movement in the forest. I rested on a blanket, my head in Rhino's lap. The big man stroked my hair whispering soothing words. His large hands were surprisingly gentle and his massive, protective presence was soothing. I dozed a little, and

Rhino woke me at intervals to check the area around us. I sent a low-level emotional sensing out into the night, to see if there were any high emotions nearby, but as the night wore on, I sensed nothing.

More people landed, I would wake with each wave of people, every time thinking the noise they make had to be heard by someone, but the night remained still.

Only twice, while we waited, did I have to reach out to some being, whose emotions had spiked, and clam it once more. I didn't even know if they were people or not. The reports were unclear as to whether the Thraians had made it to this part of the forest yet.

Then everyone was ashore, nearly a thousand people, and I rose. We would walk through the night, trying to get as far from the lake as possible before morning. I was exhausted, and in truth, I only made it perhaps a half mile before I collapsed and Rhino had to carry me.

By dawn, we were well away from the lake and the group of us rested. We hoped we were safe.

Ceph and Falcon returned from their scouting. They hadn't seen anyone following us.

It seemed, at least for now... we'd managed to get this group safely away.

I thanked all the Spirits for their blessings on this, then collapsed into sleep.

CHAPTER 15

DAWN

Swift had carried me, flying as fast as he could, in hopes of catching up with the carriage carrying Prince Estian. But swifts were not meant to carry a load as large as a small rodent. My avatar weighed as much as his did. So, he had to rest frequently. Even so, we managed to keep well ahead of Lyran and Pan, who were on horseback, riding hard somewhere behind us.

But it wasn't enough.

We reached Surrin Town and hadn't seen the carriage. It was mid-morning and the outpost commander had said the carriage would probably get here early morning. We'd failed.

I cursed our luck.

We found a place to hide and get some rest while we waited for Lyran and Pan. We weren't going to go into town without them. That would just be adding stupidity to failure. I woke to the sound of horses nearby. Swift and

I had been off the road in a thicket of brush at the edge of a copse of trees. I blinked, nudging Swift and rose. An exhausted looking Lyran and Pan were approaching.

"No luck," Lyran said; it wasn't a question. He could see we didn't have the prince. He slid off his horse and collapsed to sit with a heavy huff. "Any plans so far?" he asked head in hands.

Pan dismounted and similarly slumped to the ground. I wasn't feeling that much better than how they looked, even with the bits of sleep I'd gotten.

"Nothing. You know your brother. How would he deal with Prince Estian?"

"Aaghar is ruthless and cunning. He'll kill the prince soon enough, but not before he's wrung everything he needs out of the man. I'd give Estian... a day, no more, before he's dead, having told Aaghar everything he knows." He looked up at the sun. It was late in the day; the sun was well on its way to the horizon in the west. "That gives us tonight to get him out, and even then, we might be too late."

Calm, Dawn. I can feel you tensing. Remember what you told me. You may be bold and radical, but you plan first. Amya was right.

I drew in several long breaths. That helped to clear my mind a little.

Frist things first. "Do any of us know anything about this town?" I asked.

Swift nodded. "I did a bit of reconnaissance while you were sleeping this morning. I'm guessing Basia was never threatened from the north. The town has no walls. Even the keep only has a stone wall a dozen feet tall or so. And the keep is more of an estate, looks like it was built for pleasure, not war or defense. I saw a dragon sleeping in the yard of the estate, so the dragon lord *is* here. The manor house itself is large, and there are several outbuildings. We'd have to split up to search it all in one night."

"We'll want to stick together, or remain in groups of two at least, to watch each other's backs," I said. I didn't want us separating. We couldn't risk any of us being captured as well. The point was to get the prince out while keeping ourselves safe. I turned to Lyran. "You mentioned all the dragon lords have some ability. Yours is to camouflage yourself. What is Aaghar's?"

"His is supernatural strength. None of us could ever compete with him for raw power. He can punch clean through stone walls without hurting his fist. He can lift a full-grown ox in each hand. I've seen him hit a man with just a flick of his finger and not only kill the man but send him flying dozens of feet."

"Sounds lovely. Let's not fight him if we don't have to," Pan grumbled.

I agreed with that sentiment.

"But... that means he doesn't have any super-senses or ways of knowing we're there? Good."

"His senses will be enhanced, like mine," Lyran said. "That's a general side effect of bonding with a dragon, but as long as we're careful that should be easy enough to avoid."

"So, we rest for now," I said, thinking a plan out loud. "Go in after dark. Carefully search the estate and... We have to assume Aaghar will be with Estian, or at least have him under heavy guard. What then? How do we get past them without alerting others?"

"If my brother is with him..." Lyran shook his head. "Then... I don't know. We can't fight him, not directly. He could kill any of us with a single punch." Lyran looked at me. "If it came to a fight, you'd probably have the best chance against him. You're quick, and your spirit-gift allows you to see what others are doing before they do it. But I still wouldn't want to risk it."

Neither did I.

Pan piped up. "I'm pretty tough, I might be able to take a few of his hits."

Lyran nodded. "True, but we don't know how many hits and Aaghar has been training relentlessly in combat for more than ten years. Best not to risk it."

Pan sighed and nodded.

Lyran continued. "If it's just a few guards, I think we can deal with them quick enough, before they raise an alarm."

"The trick then will be getting out before anyone finds those guards," Swift added.

It sounded like we had a plan, if a rough one. So, we waited for dark, then made our way into the town.

With his camouflage ability, Lyran went over the

estate's wall first. He'd told us to wait while he scouted. We sat in the shadow of the wall, huddled closed. Lyran returned after what seemed like an eternity — though the moon hadn't shifted far in the sky — to tell us he'd figured out the guard rotation around the grounds and now was the time to sneak in.

Pan would wait here. If we failed and were captured or killed, someone had to get back to the others and let them know they'd need to disperse from that camp as soon as possible. If we weren't out by morning, we probably weren't coming out. As much as he didn't like it, he knew he didn't have any good way to go unseen inside. The rest of us did.

The wall was only a dozen feet tall. Swift Flew. I jumped. Lyran was able to leap high enough to catch the top and climb over.

Swift flew ahead. The rest of us crept, low and fast across the large lawns, from one small group of decorative trees to another, then to the estate. We forced open a window and slipped into a large sitting room of some sort, thankfully empty at this time of night.

So far, so good.

From here we'd try to make our way down, assuming any 'dungeon' or similar location would be underground. We'd walk openly and rely on my hearing. If we heard people coming our options were to duck into a room or for me and Swift to veer and Lyran to hold us, hiding us behind him while he blended into the walls. We could also just keep walking as if we were meant to be here, if we thought we could muster and bluster our way through.

We slipped out of the room we were in and began our search.

The guards inside were not paying attention to much, leaning on the walls, looking at each other, talking in voices which could be heard — at least by me — far down adjoining halls. We avoided them well enough.

Finding stairs, we made our way down. In the basement, we found storerooms for supplies, off dark, stone halls. Swift veered and flew to sit on Lyran's shoulder while I led Lyran along using my exceptional night vision and hearing.

My heart was racing, pounding so loud I felt like everyone in the estate had to hear it.

You're doing well, keep calm, but keep alert. I know you can make it through this. Amya was trying to be reassuring but sounded as frightened as I was.

I stopped us at an intersection of halls. There was a flickering of light down one of the perpendicular hall-ways. I listened and heard soft whispers, but... more than that, I heard a deep, commanding voice, sounding as if coming from some distance away. Then... a softer voice... Estian's!

We'd found him.

But I was nearly certain Aaghar was with the man. I relayed this to Lyran, who cursed.

He knelt next to me. "What do we do," he whispered, close, hot breath upon my ear. It sent a warm thrill through me, but... now wasn't the time for that. "Go in and fight, or wait for Aaghar to come out?"

Turning to him, I could see the uncertainty in his eyes.

I was aware of the repercussions of both options. If we waited, Estian might be breaking right now, spilling everything on Lyran and our camp. We needed to stop him from talking as soon as possible... but fighting Aaghar... was not something any of us wanted to do.

Then an ear-piercing, high-pitched scream rang out. It was definitely the prince.

Lyran twitched and made to head around the corner to wherever the prince might be, but I stopped him. "No, wait."

"What?"

"As long as the prince is screaming, he's still alive, and as long as he's screaming, he's holding out. They wouldn't be torturing him if he'd already given them the information they want to know."

Lyran blinked, seemingly thinking about this. Then he nodded. "But what if he tells them because of this torture?"

I grimaced. "I don't—"

I heard the screeching hinges of a door opening and a deep voice laughing, clearer now.

"Hide us, Aaghar is coming!" I hissed.

CHAPTER 16

LYRAN

Dawn shifted into her small rodent form and then hopped up into my hand. I put her behind my back as Swift dropped into my other hand and I did the same with him. Then I shifted down the hall a little to the shallow indentation where a door sat in this heavy stone wall. I concentrated on my camouflage, stilling my breathing. I'd look like the door behind me, wood and shadows.

Then I heard the heavy foot falls of my brother, and his chuckle — he always did find hurting others to be funny — as he came around the corner, carrying a torch.

He was larger than I remembered. He'd always been the largest of my ten brothers, as tall as Rhino, but with a more sculpted physique, and long locks of dark hair. Just seeing him filled me with an intense dread. I knew I was hidden, but as much as my mind knew it would be nearly impossible for him to see me, I couldn't stop thinking about what would happen if he did. One strike from one of his supernaturally enhanced fists and I'd be dead. And that would be the best possible outcome if he did find me. If he grabbed me, I'd not be able to escape, I'd be captured and then I'd be the one being tortured. And if he captured me... would he find Dawn and Swift? Would they get away?

Despite trying to keep myself calm, my heart just kept beating faster and harder as my brother approached along the hallway. I was gritting my teeth with the effort not to make a sound. Sweat seemed to pour out of me.

Aaghar passed me.

I eased out a sigh of relief. Aaghar stopped. Had he heard my sigh?

He half turned, looking over his shoulder, back down the hall, but... oddly, he'd turned away from me, not toward me. He stood there for a moment, then breathed a laugh and whispered: "She's going to love this." Then he continued laughing as he turned back and continued down the hall.

This time, I waited until he was well out of sight before I allowed myself to breathe again, and I found myself huffing out a long breath, shoulders falling as bunched tension finally released. We'd done it.

I brought out Dawn and Swift. "I think we're good," I whispered. And they both shifted, moving off my hands.

"I could feel your tension and fear," Dawn said. She put a hand on my arm. "Thank you for protecting us."

I smiled; glad it was over. "Anytime." Though I hoped

I'd not have to face my brother again any time soon. I knew... someday, I'd have to face him. But I wanted to be ready with a plan to deal with his massive strength. I didn't know what that would be, but I knew I'd need to have something ready, or I'd be in the same situation, where he could kill me with one blow.

Putting that from my mind, we all readied our weapons and moved back to the corner.

Dawn pointed to herself then me, "Hide," she breathed. Then she pointed around the corner and indicated we should sneak up on the guards. She and I would be able to get close before we attacked. Hopefully they'd not be able to let out an alarm.

I nodded.

I cloaked myself in my camouflage as she veered. She snuck around the corner, and I moved with her. I could move at a decent pace while hidden in this way, my masking constantly adjusting to keep me hidden.

There were only two guards — thank The Sacred Flame for that — and I went to the other side of the far one as I watched the small kangaroo-rat scurry along the base of the wall unseen by the guards. She was close. Then I waited. When she attacked so would I.

She appeared in her human form and lashed out, quickly taking her guard across the throat with her blade. I didn't even drop my camouflage as I did the same with the other guard.

They both collapsed, neither making a sound other than the clank of their armor hitting the stones.

I appeared and we nodded to each other.

I plucked up a lantern from a hook on the wall as Dawn took the keys off the belt of one of the guards.

She opened the door, and I peaked in.

"What?" Estian said sounding alarmed. "So soon? I thought..." he trailed off seeing us.

"You thought what?" I asked as I moved into the room.

Estian looked rough. His shirt had been torn away and bruises and cuts marred his pale face and torso. The real damage though, was to his hand. Three fingers on one hand had been utterly crushed, destroyed. That was definitely Aaghar's work.

"I thought... you were never going to come!" he hissed. "Get me out of here!"

"Yes, your highness," I said, as if I wasn't a prince myself, even if I was in exile.

Dawn cut his bindings and helped him to his feet. "Can you walk?" she asked.

"Yes, of course," he said hotly. "My legs are fine." He pushed her away and demonstrated. He was weak, I could tell that much, but he managed a swaying walk. "What took you so long?" he asked. Then: "How did you find me?"

"All questions for once we're well away from here," I said. "Now keep quiet your highness, and we'll have you safe soon enough."

He nodded stiffly.

We moved slowly, partially to take care while sneaking through the estate, partially because of the prince's enfeebled condition. When we'd made it back to the dark sitting room where we'd entered, we stopped for a moment. I found a stash of alcohol and poured a cup of some dark liquid. I handed it over to the prince, who took it with his good hand.

"No food, yet, but this should fortify you a little until we can get some," I said. He nodded.

Taking a long swig, he breathed a heavy sigh. "Can you believe this?" he said lifting his broken hand. "That brute... he just... squeezed and..."

"But you didn't tell him anything?" Dawn asked.

"No, of course not, what do you take me for?"

Neither of us said anything; he wouldn't have liked our answers.

"Can we go now?" Estian asked petulantly. He put the empty cup down. "I do feel better, thank you."

I'd never heard him thank me before. That was new. Perhaps this experience had changed him.

We checked the window. Swift shifted and slipped out, scouting the yard. He returned quick. "The guards have just passed; we can go now."

We moved stealthily back over the yard, moving from one group of carefully planted, decorative trees to another, then to the wall.

"Apologies for the indignity, your highness," Dawn said, then plucked the man up into her arms and leapt over the wall. Estian let out a clipped cry.

I was over quick enough, and Swift was already on the other side.

Pan beckoned us to the shadowed alley in which he hid, across from the wall. We used the rest of the night to hurry away from the town. But knowing my brother could take to the skies and spy us if we were out in the open, we hid after daybreak, resting in a thick pack of trees well off the north road.

And indeed, I did hear the bellowing call of a dragon several times that day, from various distances away. But it seemed he hadn't found us. We'd made it away safely. I thanked The Sacred Flame for that.

A week later, the group of us were safely back at the camp deep in the Maraslad Forest. We'd moved slowly, at night, and not seen any sign of my brother at all.

I couldn't quite believe our luck.

And our luck only improved when, a couple days later, Roo returned to us, leading a column of a thousand refugees. Dawn was ecstatic to see her, just as we six men, who had been caught up in the orbit of these two amazing women, were also thrilled to be all together once again.

The six of us planned something special for our two precious women, a reunion they would not soon forget.

CHAPTER 17

ROO

My body tingled all over with the anticipation of what was to come, or maybe it was the brisk river water in which I was bathing. Not far from the — now sprawling — camp beneath the heavy foliage of the Maraslad Forest, was a river. A small ridge, which ran north of the camp, caused enough of a waterfall in the river to make a nice showering spot. Other than a little froth from the waterfall, the pool was clear and clean, and you could see all the pebbles beneath the rippling waters. Dawn and I played and washed, enjoying simply being together once more. I hadn't realized how much I'd missed her until I'd seen her again. It was like we were twin halves of the same spirit — as represented by us taking the same avatar form — and we rejoiced in being whole once more.

We were also thrilled with expectation for the joining which we'd soon experience. It had been Ceph's idea:

instead of us women sneaking off into the woods with one or two men, we'd have a moment all together.

It hadn't even been a full day since I'd arrived at the camp with the refugees from Osera. Lyran, a master of planning, had seen to the disposition of the refugees and found others in the camp to help welcome them. We had sent two pigeons to Lucjan, in case they needed to contact us, but also to let them know their civilians were safe and how to get to us if they needed to flee their island. And once all of those responsibilities had been taken care of, it had been late in the evening. We'd slept... with the promise that today, our guys would be pampering and pleasuring us... all day. And I was more than a little excited to be with them all at once.

"Have you done anything like this before?" I asked Dawn.

"Spirits, no. It was thrilling enough when I was with Lyran, Pan, and Swift at the same time, I can't quite imagine both of us with all of them... all together."

Indeed, as lusty as I had been in my previous lives, I've never been with six men at once, this will definitely be a new experience for me. Leoa's tone was excited and tingling with the same anticipation I felt. One of the reasons Lumani Bonded with people was to experience new physical sensations and experiences. This would definitely be something new and wild.

The thought of being with all our men was just a bit mind-bending, but also exceedingly exciting. My body was already warmed by the thought of so much love. So much so, that I didn't mind the crisp cold river waters.

"Six at once doesn't seem possible," Dawn breathed. "I mean, I only have three holes and two hands."

I shouldn't have been shocked by her crude words, but I was, just a little. Still, I laughed. "That's good, it leaves one for me."

Dawn guffawed at that and slapped me playfully. "Like you only want one."

She was right. "They're all so... amazing," I said with a bit of awe. "I haven't been with Pan, but if he's like the others, then I'm sure he's amazing too. Rhino is large and so caring... until he gets that hungry look in his eyes, then he's a beast and... ohhhh..." I squirmed remembering when Ceph had allowed Rhino to be fully inside me. "Lyran is strong and sure, somehow taking what he wants while giving everything you need. Swift and Falcon are the same, but different, both alive with life and curiosity and passion, not to mention those heavy cocks."

"Yeah, it's like they're sporting something meant for a larger man. Like they haven't fully grown into their cocks yet. Like a baby tiger with massive paws."

I laughed. "Exactly!"

"What's Ceph like?" she asked.

"Ohhhh, he's wonderful. The way he can manipulate your body, it's amazing. He can make you feel things so deeply, it's unlike anything I've ever felt before." I returned the question. "And Pan?"

"Oddly he's not large or special when it comes to sex,

but he's dedicated and loving and for me... he's a perfect fit. When he's inside me, it just feels so... right. He doesn't need special powers to make me tingle all over."

"He sounds perfect."

"He is. I'm a bit sorry I waited to be with him."

Curious I asked. "And how have you been handling Lyran's... size?"

Dawn laughed. "I handle it very well, if I do say so myself. He's more than satisfied with my tiny pussy. Besides there are other ways I can pleasure him. And he hasn't complained about anything yet." She went silent for a moment and when I looked at her, there was a slightly cross-eye, glazed-over look in her eyes.

"Dawn?"

"I was just remembering. I have felt him fully inside me, but not inside me physically." This was intriguing. I was curious what she meant. "I was... lost in my own mind for a while — part of a long story I'll tell you later — but when Lyran came to get me out, he... connected with my spirit. He was... merged with me. Then I brought Pan and Swift into my spirit as well. We had some... interesting spirit-sex, and it was like nothing I — or they — had ever felt before. They were each a perfect fit, plunged deep into my spirit and... ah... yeah, we all had some rather awkward physical reactions to that amazing moment."

I was a bit agog. Spirit-sex? I couldn't even quite imagine what she was talking about, but given her tone... it sounded like it was on another level of bliss than physical sex. "I'll... have to try that some time... if I can."

Oh, yes please! Leoa was practically begging. *We Spirits of The Mists don't procreate like you physical creatures do, but we don't even have anything like spirit-sex either. I'd love to know what that's like.*

"We'll find a way for you to try it," Dawn said with a heavy sigh and a sloppy grin. Then she blinked and laughed again. "But yeah, getting back to Lyran's physical form... Spirits he is big. Thankfully he's not as thick as Rhino, but he's nearly as long." She sounded curious herself when she asked: "And Rhino, has he talked to you about being your 'master' yet?"

"Master? No. Why?" This was a curious turn of phrase. I didn't much care for one party being superior in sex. I liked a mutual give and take. But... I'd try anything... once.

Me too, Leoa purred.

"No reason. I did hear something from Falcon though, that Ceph did something that made you able to take him fully?" She sounded a bit awed and curious.

"Oh yes, how did Ceph put it? 'Let's move all those pesky vital organs out of the way!' Or something like that. He rearranged me inside so Rhino could fit, and oh wow, did he fit."

"Sounds painful."

"Not at all. It was glorious... amazing... I don't have the words for it."

"Truly? Wow." I saw her shudder at the thought.

"Wow, yes, that is the word. That is exactly the word."

Dawn laughed. "Maybe Ceph can do that for me too?"

"You'll have to ask. I'm sure he would."

"Spirits..." Dawn breathed. "If Rhino was... he'd be practically under my tits!"

"Yeah," I said, remembering the feeling of him so deep inside me. I rubbed my stomach and shivered with bliss at the memory.

"I think we've made them wait long enough," Dawn said, coming out from under the falls.

"I think we have." I followed her, my anticipation only growing. We stood on large rocks at the banks of the river, drying ourselves. Dawn put on a sheer silken dress that laced up the front, very provocative. She used her Fey powers over cloth to have the dress lace itself quickly, drawing it tight to her lithe form.

I had purchased some items with the funds Lusine had given us. Most had been functional travelling clothes, but I had found shop which sold the most divine silks and purchased an outfit that made me feel like the goddess Falcon and Swift claimed I was. It was of crimson, setting off the dark honey of my skin. The top draped over my large bust, hanging open beneath. It had probably been made for someone with a smaller bust and might have hung lower on them. On me it only barely covered my ample swells and depending on how I shifted my shoulders might even allow a peek at the bottom of my breasts. The separate skirt was loose and free, falling to just below my knees, with a silken tie for a belt to keep it tight where it sat, low on my hips.

We both put cloaks over our garments and wore our heavy boots as we made our way back to the camp.

The guys had bathed earlier and told us to go off and take our time while they set up our 'pavilion.'

The twins found us and escorted us away from the main camp, Swift coming to me, and Falcon taking Dawn's arm. A rough trail had been strewn with many colorful flowers, and it led to an area which had been hung with many different cloths and tarps. Entering the area — the twins pushing the draped cloths aside — we found an amazing clearing. I don't know how much work this had taken, but the ground had been cleared of brush and leveled. The trees around had been hung with the cloths and tarps, blocking it from outside sight. We removed our boots as the 'floor' had been covered with layers of blankets, creating a soft layer over the entire area. The top was simply the heavy boughs and branches of the trees, otherwise open to the sky.

"Where did you get all this cloth?" Dawn asked. I was curious too.

Lyran — already stark naked and gorgeous, since he had no issues with modesty — answered, "Some came from the refugees we brought from Basia, some from the Njorvasoturi, some from those Roo brought from Osera. Everyone has been very thankful for what we've done and wished to help make you two... comfortable."

"This is amazing," I said, and undid the clasp of my

cloak, Swift taking it from my shoulders. Dawn did the same.

The men gasped as we revealed ourselves, six sets of eyes going wide with piqued desire as they roamed both of our forms. When we'd arrived, I'd been aware — through my spirit-gift — of the warm love emanating from all of the guys, as well as a building desire and hunger. Those feeling spiked as they caught sight of our dresses. Lyran breathed out a heavy breath as I saw that long cock rise to a rigid state.

"So," Dawn said. "What do you have planned for us?" Her tone was coy, mock-innocent.

My own excitement and anticipation spiked then. I didn't know what would happen, but I wanted to find out.

Rhino and Lyran moved to the center of the area and beckoned us forward. The other men formed a rough circle around us, pressing close. For a moment, it was just that, a press of bodies, Dawn and I back-to-back. Then hands began to reach and caress. Rhino, Ceph, and Swift were closest to me, caressing me and reaching past me. And I felt some hands from others reaching past Dawn to me as well, it was an intricate web of arms and bodies. I lost track of whose hands were whose, but I knew Ceph's because wherever he touched, I felt lines of tingling-fire.

Dawn gasped. "Oh! What is that? Pan?"

I couldn't see the small man somewhere behind me, but I heard his laugh. "It turns out I have a spirit gift. Eona had thought she felt something, but we couldn't figure out what it was. Then... oddly for some time now, while near Swift, I could feel some connection to Falcon. It turns out... I can borrow the gifts of others, and this is Ceph's gift."

"Spirits, that's amazing!" Dawn said, and I heard her heavy breathing accompanying the words. I was happy for her; it meant she could get all the benefits of being with Ceph but didn't have to ask the man anything awkward since he only wanted to be with me.

This heavy press and caress continued for some time, men shifting, kneeling, ensuring we were touched... everywhere. Arms and legs were massaged to a warm, relaxed state, hair was combed and stroked. Careful fingers traced my face, lightly, gently, brushing over my lips, forming to the curve of my cheek and ear, even tenderly stroking my eyelids over closed eyes. I wanted nothing more than some of those fingers to find my folds, but for that... they waited. I was trembling with a peaceful, balmy bliss before any man even kissed me!

Ceph was the first to find my lips and — as suspected — he left them tingling with increased sensitivity after only a soft brush of his mouth. I moaned as he plucked at my bottom lip. My core ached with slick fire, yearning to be touched. Still, they took their time.

While Ceph kissed my face and lips, Rhino's large hands took a firmer approach to my breasts, still over my silken dress, but that didn't matter, the fabric only served to enhance the feel of the heavy, rough hands. Swift knelt and I let out a long keening moan as finally, strong hands slid up the inside of my thigh to brush my folds. And when deft fingers found my slick heat, I gasped into Ceph's lips. I continued to gasp and moan as Swift explored my wet folds, up into my curls, then brushed my clitoris lightly.

Similar things must have been happening with Dawn, as I heard her gasps of pleasure and felt her body tremble against my back. I reached out with my gift, feeling the mounting passion among everyone here. And I too trembled, knowing there were greater heights yet to be reached.

We had only just begun.

Oh yes, Leoa moaned, and I felt her passion as well. She was practically vibrating within me, and that only made my own pleasure rise and peak. I felt an orgasm build, steady and powerful, but still distant. I trembled at how powerful it felt already. My grunts grew louder, needful. I wanted to let everyone know just how amazing a job they were doing.

Slowly, Dawn and I were turned, until my back was to Rhino, and hers to Lyran. The two large men shifted, reaching down and in to take our legs and lift us easily. Ceph continued his work with hands and lips upon my face and torso, sending thrills through me. Pan was doing the same with Dawn. Rhino and Lyran had their hands full, controlling us. They opened our legs wide to the sides. Our skirts retreated up, revealing all of us to Swift and Falcon who knelt before us like they were worshiping some goddess, and dove in with their lips upon us.

I closed my eyes, head tilted back to rest on Rhino's thick chest, simply taking in all the glorious sensations: Ceph's tingling touches and burning kisses, Swift's soft lips, flicking tongue and probing fingers. I was ready now, the orgasm throbbing through me, so near. I panted and cried out, trembling.

I could feel the same orgasmic response in Dawn, we were so strongly connected. Waves of her bliss washed out from the ocean of her soul to lap on my shores. Curious, I linked our emotions together. The combination was too much for both of us and we both let out a long, guttural, growling groan as we came in unison.

Blessed Spirits! That had been so very hot and amazing and none of us — except Lyran — were even fully naked yet!

As if reading my thoughts, Pan and Ceph broke off from their divine ministrations to stand before us. They moved slowly, sensually, removing one bit of clothing at a time. I concentrated on Ceph's long-limbed, finely muscled form. The heat in his clear blue eyes ratcheting up my arousal another notch. I could feel the barely restrained desire radiating off him, the raw need held in check. I so desperately wanted to feel it, feel him inside me. Then he was naked, and he slowly stroked his long, slender cock until it was twitching with its own powerful need.

As they moved back in, Swift and Falcon left from where they had been kneeling. Ceph and Pan took their places lips and fingers upon our folds, now stimulating us with a renewed intensity. I felt Ceph's long fingers slip inside me, touching me with intense thrill and gut-contracting pleasure. I came again, already so aroused and sent over the top by his deep and so-very-stimulating massage. And when his fingers drew out, covered in my juices, they sought my other opening, spreading my own moisture around it, as they worked that tight bud to open. It was almost too much to bear... and that's when the twins started their striptease. They worked together, removing clothes from the other, their gazes moving between Dawn and I with fiery hunger. And when they were naked, they broke out a bottle of oil and began to oil each other until their bodies glistened and their too-big cocks were slick and wet.

Rhino set me down, but supported me, since my legs were weak. Dawn was also set down and she seemed just as wobbly-legged as I was. Then, all together, sharing the moment, Rhino, Lyran, Ceph, and Pan began to remove our clothing.

Dawn, apparently impatient, moved her hand down over the laces of her dress and they undid themselves swiftly, falling away, the front of the dress opening. It was gently removed from her as she was caressed. Mine took a little longer, the belt undone, skirt smoothed down over my hips, top lifted as other hands found the sensitive skin of my breasts, the aroused nubs of my nipples and traced them tantalizingly.

The twins then lay on their backs, rubbing their oiled

cocks to twitching fullness. I felt a thrill at what was to come.

Lyran and Ceph lifted me together, and I was brought to Swift and helped to kneel astride him, facing away from him, toward his feet.

I felt Swift's well-oiled fingers slipping into my rear opening, pulling me down as he massaged me with oil. Then I felt the press of that magnificent cock of his, his hands moving to my hips, holding me, moving me ever-so-gently as he pushed slowly, carefully, into me.

And when I felt the full, hot bulge of his tip inside me, with Ceph's deft fingers upon my folds and Lyran's needful lips upon mine, I came with shocking intensity, hearing Swift grunt as I clamped down upon his cock.

Ceph's hand cupped my loins, pressing his palm and fingers hard against me, causing a second wave of bliss, before he began a vigorous stroking, thrusting into my more-than ready opening with those deft fingers.

I cried out, but my lips were covered by Lyran's, and his hands upon my breasts and back massaged me as he helped me lie back. And Swift, grunting with barely restrained passion, filled my rear entrance, pushing deep as I sat, then lay back, upon him.

"Spirits!" Dawn was whispering over and over again as — I assumed — something similar was happening with her.

Then Ceph and Lyran shifted, Lyran moving between my legs. That long cock of his was throbbing and red —

as hot as the look in his indigo eyes — as he pressed it to my wetness.

"Get ready," Ceph whispered as he nibbled my ear, one of his hands moving over my belly and I felt that same... 'opening' he'd done for Rhino. Meanwhile, Lyran kept his thrusts light and shallow, slipping the tip of his divine cock easily into my drenched and dripping folds.

Then Ceph licked my ear as he said "all yours" to Lyran.

And at that, Lyran grabbed my hips and thrust hard, plunging deep, fully inside me with a whimpering grunt of his own. I felt his amazed desire. He'd never been so fully inside a woman, he'd always been too big, but now... His grunting grew with the savage intensity of his thrusts, needful and long.

My head lolled to one side. What I saw next to me, through a haze of bliss-tears, was Dawn's open-mouth, silent scream, back arched, body trembling with a series of powerful orgasms as Rhino plunged fully into her. Pan must have adjusted her using Ceph's powers, and each of the massive man's thrusts shook Dawn's entire body. I would have thought it too much for her, until I heard her moan. "More... harder!"

I was trembling through a series of orgasms myself, building to something feral and powerful which I hoped would coincide with Lyran and Swift's release.

Some part of my mind remembered Ceph was being left out of this and my grasping hand sought and found his long cock, grasping it tightly before beginning a pounding stroke.

Dawn's ecstatic peak when Rhino released inside her was so powerful I felt it wash over me. And with a blissful and mischievous smile, I let it take me, fill me, and propel me up to her heights as well. Then... I shared it with all of the guys.

The clearing became a cacophony of cries and shouts, grunts and gasps. Lyran and Swift both came at once, deep inside me, filling me with their heat. Ceph's cock swelled and surged in my hand, and I felt heavy sprays of his come over my belly and breasts.

Blessed Spirits, that was... I can't... that was... Leoa had no words, and neither did I.

I felt Dawn's seeking hand pawing at my arm. I brought my hand to hers and we clasped tightly, fingers interlocking as we rode the waves of this inhuman ecstasy to its final, twitching throes.

And that's when it started all over again.

CHAPTER 18

DAWN

I WAS ALREADY PLEASURED BEYOND REASON, BEYOND SENSE and human capability. When Pan had let Rhino thrust himself fully inside me, I'd never felt so full, nor such intensity of power as a man had taken me. Each of the massive man's thrusts had lifted me, bodily, shifting me upon Falcon's cock as well, which was already filling my rear entrance to extremes. I'd watched the glazed-over, raw animal intensity in Rhino's eyes as he'd dominated me, my body shaking, mind blown with each powerful thrust.

That alone had lifted me, sent me into supernatural heights of incomparable bliss, which I'd known only once before, during spirit-sex. And accordingly, my orgasm had been just as transcendently strong when I'd felt the warm and heavy rush of his release, low in my chest.

I thought I cried out, "Yes, master!" but I wasn't

entirely certain because even as I rose on the heights of that heavenly orgasm... I'd felt my own bliss washing back upon me and flowing through all the others in a second mind-blowing orgasm as Roo had shared it with us all once more.

And now I lay, trying to catch my breath. Rhino still resting, impossibly deep inside me. Falcon's final twitches and pulses filling me even more.

Spirits and Sprites, that was the most amazing sex I've ever had in all my lifetimes! Amya was near to shouting, ecstatic.

"Are you...?" Rhino said, as he found his breath. His feral passion fading, replaced with concern. "Did I...?"

"You... destroyed me... Rhino," I said between gasps for air. "I will... never... be the same... again." And it was partly the truth. I wasn't sure I'd ever be the same after feeling his too-deep and inhumanly powerful thrusts.

His eyes flared wide with concern... before he realized I was joking and gave a soft laugh. But laughing made his cock twitch, and that made me twitch with a surge of bliss. I laughed with him, between mini-orgasms.

Once we'd all come down enough, we rested for a moment.

Rhino pulled out of me, and Pan put me back to normal. Then I was rolled onto my side so Falcon could pull out from me, deliciously slowly. "That was divine," he whispered in my ear, voice hot. "You're still a goddess in my books."

I love him... I love all of them! You are the luckiest woman who ever lived, Amya purred.

I had to agree as I lay on my back, staring up at the branches and blue sky, still trying to fully comprehend what had just happened.

Roo was next to me. Ceph lay next to her, stroking her as Pan did the same with me.

The others left and returned with armloads of food, including several pitchers of cool water. The trays of food included: hearty meats, sharp cheeses, crusty bread, and fresh berries. We all ate and drank, restoring ourselves.

I know I don't have a stomach, but I feel like I could eat a horse after that rough exercise, Amya said, and I agreed, delving into the delightful tastes.

And our men, between mouthfuls of food, found mouthfuls of us ladies as well. It was a slow, soft, sensual thing, worshiping us with their mouths and delicate-tracing fingers upon all parts of our bodies. Pan and Ceph remained with their designated woman, instilling tingling fire wherever they touched, but all of the rest, moved around like we two women were a part of this buffet, and these men were anxious to partake of every part. Falcon sucked on my toes, and kissed my feet, whispering blessings to his 'goddess.' Swift nibbled my earlobes and kissed my hair, which was more stimulating that I might have thought. Lyran found a sensitive spot behind my knee to kiss and blow hot breath upon. Rhino kissed every finger, then my palm, and a divine spot on the inside of my wrist, before making his way up my arm to other parts. They moved between Roo and I, keeping us at a pleasant level of arousal.

I truly felt... worshiped, adored and divine.

Amya was silent, just savoring the delight of this strange meal.

And once I'd had my fill and rested a bit more, Pan shifted, moving between my legs. From the corner of my eye, I caught Ceph doing the same with Roo. Ceph and Pan had been mostly left out of the last round. They'd still had a release, but only from Roo's sharing of orgasmic emotion. "We'll take it slow," he said softly to me. "I know you're full."

"Not full enough, not until you're inside me too," I whispered to him. He smiled, a steamy hunger in his amethyst eyes. His gaze held mine as his fingers traced my folds. I was already sensitive and aroused, and now added to that was the pleasant thrill of warm tingling from his power, which blossomed into me. I was very quickly a moaning pile of putty in his hands. He kept his hands upon me as I felt his cock slip easily inside. After the pounding Rhino had given me, I felt loose and open, but then I felt my body shift, close in and constrict. Suddenly his cock was my entire world, filling me fully as I clamped tightly around him.

"Yes, all you," I moaned. "Only you. So full!"

His thrusts were slow and long, actually drawing completely out of me as he took his time pleasuring me, his fingers still thrilling me with every aching touch and when they brushed my clitoris, I couldn't help but orgasm.

The other men, kept moving between Roo and me, feasting upon our parts as Ceph and Pan slowly brought us to one trembling, fiery orgasm after another with their patient, leisurely thrusts and magical fingers. And by the time Pan finally began to thrust in earnest — grabbing my hips, raising and tilting them, drawing my legs together to rest on his shoulder as he sought his release — I was lost to this world. I had been so elevated by a series of orgasms that my body had gone from tense and twitching to relaxed and weightless. I felt like I was floating, a being of pure sensation and feeling. I felt grasping hands on my hips, the thrust of a perfect cock, as well as the many kisses and caresses all over and it was wonderful. And when Pan grunted and I felt his warm release, there came a shooting sensation of additional pleasure, straight from my hips to my head and I cried out. I needed him to know how amazing it felt to feel him come.

Roo was right there with me, also calling out her wordless praise for her man's devoted attentions.

Pan collapsed beside me, and we kissed and nibbled each other for a long moment of playful bliss.

I was delirious with pleasure. I took food and water when it was offered to me, but I was barely aware of my surroundings.

Someone whispered: "Dawn, do you wish for more, or a rest?"

"More," I said dreamily. "Always more."

Then I was moving, shifting, sitting. Hands moved over me, helping me, guiding me, and caressing me as I came to straddle a man. My eyes focused long enough to see one of the twins below me as I was lowered upon his thick cock, and it filled my pussy wonderfully. Then, a smaller cock was pushing in my other opening, a cock which sent thrills through me with the slightest touch, and to which I opened quickly and easily... that must be Pan using his tricks. I was kept upright, Pan kneeling behind me with soft thrusts while I rocked myself upon Swift's cock.

"Would you like another?" a deep voice rumbled from above me. I looked up seeing a large figure standing next to me. I blinked, bringing my eyes to focus on Lyran, his cock presented before me. I smiled as I reached up and took it, stroking it, bringing it to my lips. I took him deep into my mouth, feeling the rigid flesh brush the back of my throat, then slide deeper still. I felt like I should be choking, but this felt natural, and when my lips came to his base, my eyes fluttered open as he let out a curse: "Blessed Flames of the heavens!" Then he gave a couple short thrusts. This couldn't be. I should be choking, but then, as Pan kissed my back and hair and shoulders, I recalled his ability — borrowed from Ceph — to manipulate me. I reached around Lyran grabbing his hard butt and forced him just that little bit deeper, moving my head and throat around him. I felt him shudder, his hands on my head as he cursed again. Then I felt the pulsing, surging warmth of his release in my throat before he pulled out, staggering back, eyes wide, still cursing up a storm. I winked at him, licking my lips.

I think all of that was a bit too much for the other two men with me. Their thrusting grew frantic. Pan brought his hands up to my breasts and grabbed them, forcefully, covering my sensitive orbs with his thrilling energy. I was alive with ecstasy; every fiber of my being was burning with bliss, and I felt like I exploded inward and out. At the same time, two other explosions of warmth blossomed within me.

I think I blacked out then. I'd never blacked out from excess of pleasure before, but I did that time.

I woke to evening falling. A blanket had been laid over me and I felt... so serene and fulfilled and wonderful.

"Hello there, my personal daybreak," Pan whispered next to me. He was laying on his side watching me as I woke. "You are the most wonderous and beautiful woman the world has ever known. He reached over to brush a wayward strand of hair behind my ear. There was no special thrill to this touch this time, but it was still soft and caring. "Are you well?" he asked, a bit concerned. "We were all a little afraid when you passed out."

"Too much pleasure, far more than anything I'd ever felt before and I think my mind just shut down, it couldn't take such extremes of bliss. No, there is nothing wrong, I feel amazing." I quickly added, "You are amazing. You're all amazing!"

He leaned down to kiss me softly before resuming his side-lying position.

"How is Roo?" I asked.

He looked away, to some other area of the clearing. "She is... a font of affection and love." There was a certain awe in his voice. "I can see why the others love her as they do. Even I love her" — he looked back at me and smiled — "but not like I love you. Nothing can compare with that."

Curious, I propped myself up on my arms to look where Pan had looked. Though, even before I saw her, I felt her. Love radiated out to me, into me, through me.

Oh! Amya gasped, filled with awe and beauty at what I saw.

Roo was dancing.

CHAPTER 19

CEPH

I WAS MESMERIZED. ALL OF US WERE.

Roo had risen after a playful and lazy round of plea-suring, with all five of us making her feel — what we'd hoped was — wonderful and loved and beautiful. Perhaps this was her way of showing us her appreciation? She hadn't said a word, just begun to dance, and we'd all quieted, sitting around her, watching, enwrapped and entranced.

This is... for once Ulio, my bizarre Lumani was quiet, speechless. I was thankful for that. I could just enjoy the show.

Her movements were slow and swaying, eyes closed, mouth in a faint smile as she moved. She flowed and twirled, stepping lightly, seemingly caught up in her own bliss. Her arms floated, weightless, sometimes at her sides, sometimes combing up through her auburn hair until it fell back down in waves, as her arms swayed above her head. The graceful steps were a pure expression of love and joy; her love for us, and her joy at our love for her. I didn't know how I knew this, other than that it was expertly communicated through Roo's slow and rhythmic movements.

I was aroused; how could I not be with this beautiful and sensual woman dancing naked before me, but it was a distant thing to the other emotions stirred within me: my own joy and love, a grateful appreciation of this singular beauty and through that an appreciation for all that was beautiful. I was moved beyond words.

Peripherally, I saw some of the men move and I looked to see Dawn approaching. She too seemed drawn to Roo, like moth to flame. But then, once she was close enough, within our circle — made larger now with the addition of Pan — she closed her eyes and began dancing as well.

And that was a truly amazing sight: not that Dawn's dancing was better than Roo's, but that somehow, these two women, eyes closed and otherwise seemingly unaware of each other, were matching each-other's movements exactly, perfectly, twinned. Roo had told me the two of them were connected, but this display showed just how deep that connection was.

And in that transcendent moment, Roo was love personified. The elegant step of her full legs, the sway of those full round hips, the undulations of arms and careless but perfect curl and extension of her fingers were like some full-body embrace I could feel within my soul. The fading light caught her tawney, dark-honey skin and shimmered in waves upon it. And her auburn hair gleamed with ember-reds, a fire waiting to be reborn in purest flames. The rhythmic waves of her body, the swing of her full breasts, the beatific smile on her upturned face; it was like some mind-capturing drug, from which I could not escape.

And if Roo was love, then Dawn was power. The small woman seemed taller than anyone here in that moment, a towering giantess, who might carelessly step on any of us mere mortals at any moment, but we dare not run from her, for this sight, this dance, was a true and wonderful blessing. Her movements, though the same as Roo's were just a bit sharper with a precision and force to them. Her black hair flew about her, like ocean waves at night, whipped up by a storm. Roo was graceful, but Dawn was truly refined and smooth, nimble and lissome. She seemed to float, her feet not quite touching the ground, her slender form bending and arching beyond what seemed possible. Her blue-pale, porcelain skin seemed to give off its own faint light, radiant and captivating. She was truly compelling and forceful, but that was... just a bit too much for me. I preferred Roo's softer, more down-to-earth dance of love and compassion.

When the two of them heard the last note of whatever mystical music they danced to, they stopped in perfect poise and pose. All of us men cheered and clapped and shouted. It wasn't enough. There would never be enough adulations for what we had just experienced.

This moment would be burned into my soul and mind. I would always find solace in this memory, for the rest of my life, I knew it. I wept openly and freely at the unearthly beauty of the gift I'd just been given.

I don't know if either woman knew the true depths of the effect they had just had on all of us. They laughed freely once they opened their eyes, a moment of levity and joy so pure that it too touched my soul. Then they collapsed next to each other and reached out to clasp hands in some unspoken physical need to connect.

Roo laughed. "If you had told me a year ago, that I'd be dancing naked with another woman, for an audience of naked men whom I adore, I would not have believed you."

"I... felt that. It's burned upon my spirit," Lyran said softly. "When the two of you join like that, become one in spirit and form and love and power, I... I don't think there is a force in this world that could stop you." He sighed. "That was the single most amazing moment of my life."

The rest of us murmured our agreement to this.

The women blushed, and for Dawn that made the blue-pale skin of her cheeks turn to just a hint of pale pink; a stunning change. Certainly, Pan was caught up by it. I heard his breath catch and when I looked, his erection was as stiff and as proud as it could be.

"More?" Dawn said, mischievously, seeing what I'd seen.

"If you asked me to pleasure you forever, I'd find a

way," he said softly. "I'd need no food nor water, no sleep nor activity, your love would sustain me forever more."

Dawn... blushed just a shade deeper. Her breath was just a little heavy, catching, when she said: "Show me."

Pan went to her, kneeling next to her, and reached out to cup her cheek. He stayed there, unmoving, just gazing at her for a long moment, so heated and intense were his amethyst eyes that Dawn blushed deeper again. This time it spilled down to her chest, which was heaving with quick, heavy breaths. Then Pan kissed her, gentle and soft, but deep and incredibly passionate.

"Well, what are you waiting for," Roo said. "Who's going to do that for me?"

I moved swiftly, though I needn't have. The others knew of my singular devotion for Roo.

They all love her. We all love her, but they know how you feel is even more special, Ulio said reverently.

Even you? You'll not start going on about dogwood trees or the tiny bugs that live on spiders, trying to distract me?

Indeed, I will not. At any other time, I would regale you with all of my wonderous knowledge, but now I know you must focus on her, and I wish to do the same.

Thank you.

I knelt before her, feeling the aching stiffness of my cock, and trying not to think of the throbbing need building there.

Roo, apparently, had no qualms thinking about it. Her gaze dipped down and her hand reached up to stroke me softly, gently. That only caused my erection to twitch and rise and strain and ache all the more.

"How much do you love me?" Roo asked softly. It wasn't anything selfish or needful, just curious.

"I love you more than words can say. It is impossible not to love you," I breathed. "You *are* love, and any man who doesn't love you is devoid of heart and passion. And though I cannot be certain that among all men, in all of time, I love you the most, I can say that you *are* my heart. You are my soul and spirit and I belong with you. Your pain is my pain, your joy is my joy, and I will spend the rest of my life doing everything I can to bring you the utmost of joy and bliss. I will—"

"Stop talking and show me." She reclined back, all sensual and luxurious relaxation. Her hand was still stroking me, and I was at my limit. I wove a minor manipulation within me, such that I'd remain at this point at the aching, painful pinnacle of hardened need but would not release. My body rebelled for a moment, bending, clenching needing that powerful eruption, but I stilled those tremors and moved to lie on my side next to Roo.

I leaned down and kissed her soft, yielding lips, feeling them open to me, as I sought deeper. A soft moan escaped her as I feathered a touch of a single finger low on her belly, sending tingling thrills into her.

Her hand on my cock continued a rhythmic pull, reminding me of my imminent need and I ran my finger up her belly to just below her breasts and with the movement sent powerful, sizzling bliss into every part of her, pooling lower in her loins, swelling through her chest, tingling down arms and legs and exploding in her mind. Her body arched and she gasped into my mouth.

I drew back, continuing my hard pulsing of intense pleasure into her body. Her eyes were wide, mouth gaping, her expression almost questioning as she twitched through a bliss so intense it must have felt like a thousand tidal waves crashing into her... but without any release.

"What you're feeling," I whispered. "Is what I'm feeling for you, right now. I am at my limit. I can take no more. I am caught at the moment of purest need but without a release."

She grabbed my cock, hard and I nearly doubled over with the pain-pleasure that caused. She pulled me to her, opening her legs. She had no words, but her actions spoke clear enough as she pulled me to her folds and plunged me inside.

Her eyes rolled back then, and a moment later mine did as well as her wet warmth grasped my cock and pulled me deeper. I needed to be fully inside her, I lengthened her tunnel to fit my long shaft and pressed my base into her, grinding over her clitoris. Her back arched higher, head lolling back. Her full breasts rising up to me. I sucked a full, dark areola into my mouth, flicking her rigid nipple with my tongue. At the same time, I completed one slow thrust out and back in, rocking upon her clitoris once more.

"Please..." she breathed, barely a whisper. I felt her

enfold me in her emotions, sharing her gift with me. I was drowning in love, desire, lust, need, passion, so intense it broke my mind. I cried out, as did she, unable to stop myself from thrusting harder and harder. I had to. We had to. I knew in the back of my mind that this would never end, we'd be caught up in this moment of aching, painful bliss forever... unless I used my gift to finally release us both. But her overwhelming emotions were wreaking havoc with my control.

Harder and harder, faster and more furious we built up this intense moment, our bodies lost to flailing lust.

I desperately tried to regain control as wave after torrential wave of perfect, powerful orgasmic bliss swept through and over me. I clawed and scraped and drove myself mad as I neared my breaking point.

Allow me, Ulio said softly. *As pleasurable as it might be, I do not wish for us to die like this.* He gave me just enough strength to regain a hint of control. I ripped away my restraint of our combined release, allowing Roo and I to finally, desperately erupt.

I'd never made such a feral and savage noise as I did then, and Roo's wordless cry was perhaps even more bestial than mine. I had had powerful releases before, but this one was unlike any other. I almost wondered if my cock had actually exploded, bursting so hard it had sundered itself as I twitched and pulsed inside Roo. I felt her clamp around me so hard I screamed again. She pulsed around me, milking me, wringing every drop from me, seeking the fullness of this ultimate orgasm. My balls grew painfully tight as they discharged all of their capacity into her. Even after that, our moment of release lingered, twitching and pulsing and pulling at us long after I'd run dry and she'd taken her fill.

We came down in excruciatingly small increments, as we slowly, thankfully relaxed. I fell upon her, heavy and utterly exhausted.

Neither of us even had the energy to kiss or nibble, we just lay panting. And when finally, I had withdrawn from her, I had to look, had to check that I was still in one piece.

She giggled, a bit breathless. "I know," she said. "It felt like you truly had burst inside me. Are you still intact?"

"Yes." Thankfully I was.

In that moment, I was torn. I never wanted to feel that perfect painful pleasure again, because if I did, I might just let it kill me the next time. And yet I wanted it too, over and over until it killed me. It would certainly be the best possible way to die.

Now that you mention it... it probably would be. Perhaps I shouldn't have let you regain control. I would have loved that experience.

Shut up, Ulio.

I flopped onto my back next to her. "That was..." There weren't words.

"I know," she whispered. "With your ability with body, and mine with emotions, we're a dangerous combination."

"Dangerous and sublime," I said. "Intoxicating."

She let out a breathy laugh. "Indeed."

We rested and dozed as night fell.

Blankets were gathered and laid over us. We all remained close, the eight of us; six men pressed close to the two women we loved. And for all of us... rest was a soothing blessing that night.

That was until alarms sounded and we woke... to the forest burning around us.

CHAPTER 20

LYRAN

Lyran, wake yourself! Your brother and Thavralian are coming! Eophon's voice boomed into my mind, and I woke from a restful slumber, instantly alert. I smelled smoke and heard distant screams and shouts. The trees around our little bower weren't burning yet, but I could see a garish orange glow through the draped blankets. The sky danced with light. It would be like a beacon to my brother.

"Everyone up quickly!" I shouted. "The dragon lord has found us! We'll be attacked soon!" For a moment I wondered if the blaze had been started by Thavralian's fire, but no... Eophon had said they were coming, not here, not yet.

We dressed quickly before fleeing our bower. By that time, trees along the one side were burning. The fire seemed to be spreading quickly.

Falcon and Swift took flight to see what they could

from the air.

If a dragon hadn't started this forest fire, then... to me, that meant only one thing: sabotage. There had been no storm or lightning. There were enough people here that this might have been an accident, but a cold feeling in my gut told me it wasn't.

We encountered others, thankfully well organized, picking up the most important things from their camp and fleeing the flames, while others were being organized to go down to the river and bring water.

"What happened?" I asked one of my lieutenants.

The man's face hardened. "Prince Estian did this."

I blinked. Then I spun to Dawn. Her face was grim.

"They got to him," she hissed, eyes burning with hatred. "He's signaling the dragon lord where we are. Leading him right to us!"

We'd brought him back here only to bring our own doom.

I turned back to my lieutenant. "We have roughly thirteen hundred warriors, take a thousand and prepare to face the army in the forest. The rest will help get as many of the refugees away from this place."

The man nodded and went to work.

"What can we do?" This from a hard female voice. It drew my attention and I looked to see Astraed with several Njorvasoturi.

"If you heard my command to my man, do the same. Some of us must survive to carry on the fight. Get as many as you can to safety. If I or the others with me don't survive the night, head east to Elista."

"Tell them Dawn and Roo sent you. My mother the queen will take you in and help you," Dawn said swiftly.

Astraed wasted no time on meaningless words but was quickly in motion, spreading the command to her folk.

Falcon and Swift landed nearby.

"We've been betrayed," Falcon said.

"Yes, we know. Estian." Dawn spat the man's name.

Swift added: "A dragon is approaching from the south." As if to punctuate those words, a far-off dragon-cry pierced the night. We all shuddered at the slivers of fear it was meant to induce. Swift continued, "There's an army moving through the woods. They'll be here soon enough." To Dawn he added. "Swan is with them."

She swore.

Dawn had mentioned the name in passing, an enemy, but I knew little else. It didn't matter, I knew what I had to do. "I must keep you all safe," I said. "I'll bring Eophon and face my brother. The only chance we have is dragon to dragon. If I can unseat him high enough the fall will kill him."

Dawn and Roo both came to me. Roo pulled me down, going to tip toes to kiss my cheek. Dawn had to jump to wrap her arms around me to kiss the other. "Be safe," they said as one.

I nodded and left them there to sprint through the woods.

Eophon to me! Tonight, we fight!

I have heard the challenge from my consanguine Thavralian. I come.

We met in the thick of the forest, Eophon crashing through trees to reach me. I mounted quickly, sinking into the known comfort of the dragon saddle behind Eophon's head. Then, with a leap, we were above the trees. Strong wings grappled the air and we climbed higher into the night. Eophon called, a bellowing roar, answering Thavralian's cry from earlier.

The other dragon bellowed again in reply. We had our bearing.

"Here I come, brother," I whispered. I just hoped I was ready for this. I was the youngest of the dragon riders and by default the least experienced. I'd participated in 'play' combat with my brothers, but never a true battle. I didn't know my worth, not as a true dragon rider. I would know after tonight.

Even with my enhanced senses I could see nothing, Aaghar and Thavralian were too far off still, but I smiled. They'd not be able to see me... and they never would.

Let's cloak ourselves in night, I said to Eophon and got a sense of cunning joy at the guile.

We used our powers to hide ourselves, now our foes would never see us coming. Once we were close enough, they might hear the flap of Eophon's wings, but by then it would be too late.

Thavralian is a dangerous foe, larger than I, the strongest of all dragons, of all creatures who have ever lived. Eophon didn't seemed worried, though I sensed a hint of caution from them. *We must be fast, hit and hide, it will take us several passes, but we can do it.* Yet I knew, one strike from Thavralian would end this fight.

We had stealth, they had strength. We'd find out which was superior this night.

The massive shadow of Thavralian came into view ahead of us, more than three times Eophon's size.

Let's go high, take them from above first.

Yes, good idea. If we glide down to them, they shall not hear us.

Eophon tore at the air, and we climbed higher, above my brother and his dragon.

Then Eophon went still, wings outstretched to soar, staying mostly in place against the wind as Thavralian charged forward to just the right spot beneath us.

We dove.

The larger dragon's head turned at the last second, perhaps he'd caught a scent of us, but it was too late. Eophon's claws raked through Thavralian's hide where the back of the wing met the body, shredding the leathery wing and drawing long lines through the tough scales, not deep, but deep enough to hurt.

Then we were away, diving lower and banking back and forth as fire warmed the airs behind us. One strike down.

Thavralian's bellow of pain and rage made me smile. I looked behind to see the giant dragon banking slowly as they strove to climb higher into the air.

They will make us come at them from below. If they still their wings and we are climbing hard they will hear us, I noted. It was a solid plan.

If they climb high enough, which I believe they intend, then we will not be able to get above them at all.

No, but we can be level with them. Take us up, but far from them. Then we'll soar in as silent as they are and take out one of Thavralian's wings.

Yes, Eophon gave the impression of pride. *A good plan.*

Eophon took us higher, almost too high. The air grew thin, and I had to still my breathing, calling upon my spirit to sustain me as my mind began to wander a little, head aching with the pressure.

But we were level with Thavralian and as planned, Eophon fanned their wings wide and glided in close.

But Thavralian and Aaghar adjusted course just as we arrived. And since we could make no adjustments to our course for fear of making noise, we didn't get the meat of Thavralian's wing, but tore off the tip instead.

The larger dragon bellowed and blew fire at us.

We dove and wove to avoid the repercussive blasts, some close enough to singe Eophon's right wing but doing no lasting harm.

Thavralian was enraged now; he blew fire all around him.

Good, let him blow himself out! Eophon laughed.

The massive beast was also forced lower, just missing that small bit of wing was enough to hinder how well he could glide. We circled to come at them from behind. I was feeling confident now. They hadn't seen us yet, we'd gotten in two minor strikes; one good one and Thavralian would be downed, though probably still far from dead.

We got above them, more agile and faster, and dove at the dragon's long tail. But then...

Change of plans, I said quickly as the others drew near fast. *Run their back and burn my brother.* Taking out the dragon's tail would hurt it but not kill it. Taking out my brother would be far worse. And as much as dragon fire did little to other dragons, especially against their well armored hides, against a human it was deadly.

I got Eophon's acknowledgment of my plan.

We flew in from behind and banked, streaming in over the massive form of Thavralian toward my brother.

We had him!

Then Eophon bucked suddenly and went limp as something slammed into us from below. Whether from intuition or some supernatural knowing, Thavralian had bashed us with the massive spiked ball at the end of their tail.

Eophon's mind-voice was silent as we fell from the skies like a stone.

Sacred Flame, wake up my friend! Please! Eophon hear me! Eophon! I bellowed into my dragon's mind.

A slurred mental reply came back: *Lyran?*

Yes, my friend, you're falling, fly!

Fall... Falling? I... The words were still distant and hazy, Eophon was alive, but not faring well.

The ground rushed up at us, a massive darker shadow in the night.

Eophon please! Gather yourself or we'll both die!

No! This was clear, breaking through the fog of Eophon's thoughts. Wings flapped, righting us, then spread and caught wind in time to skim the tops of trees, keeping us from our doom.

Are you well, friend? I asked.

No, Lyran. That was a nasty hit. Bones are broken, my belly is torn open. I rain blood like a storm upon the forest below.

That was not a pleasant image.

Can you fight or should we hide?

I fear—

Fire blasted around us, singing my back and scorching one of Eophon's wings.

It was only then I realized we'd become visible as we'd fallen.

Hide! Now! I shouted at Eophon.

I do not know if I can. Eophon's voice was weak.

Fire blasted far too close over us, and I ducked low.

Then I heard a horrid noise from behind and Eophon cried out with such extremity of pain into my mind that it stunned me.

I blinked, trying to shake myself back to reality. Turning I saw a terrible gash in Eophon's back where massive claws had torn away scales, flesh and bone leaving a gaping hole.

Eophon, we must hide!

But Eophon didn't respond.

Eophon?

I turned back to the sound of snapping branches and breaking trees as Eophon crashed into the forest. I raised my arms to protect my face. That meant I didn't see what hit me. I know only that one moment we were tearing through the forest, nearing the ground and the next... there was only darkness and an echoing silence.

CHAPTER 21

RHINO

I STOOD READY, MASSIVE SWORD IN HAND. CEPH STOOD beside me. A line of others from Lyran's forces stood with us. We were the first and only line of defense for the hundreds of others trying to flee.

Oh Spirits, this is going to be fun! Iomu was far too happy about this dire situation.

Fun? I spat into my mind.

Oh, come on, she said. *You know you'll survive this, you're amazing! How could you not. Let's maim some baddies!*

I just shook my head.

I could hear the enemy approaching, crashing through the forest ahead of me.

"Nothing stupid this time, right?" Ceph asked.

"No promises."

That's the spirit! Iomu cheered.

Ceph gave a laugh. "I should have known."

"When it comes to the safety of Dawn and Roo and

all those others, I'll fight till you have to pull me away."
And I would.

*Oooh, yeah, badass speech. And also, I would have killed
for a man to love me like that in my previous lives!*

Ceph's tone was just a little too serious when he said:
"Yeah, but I'll be doing the same thing and may not be
able to pull you away so... try to keep yourself safe, will
you? I may need *you* to save *my* ass."

Oh.

"And," he added, "try to remember your hit and fade
technique. I think that's possibly your best weapon. Now,
if you'll excuse me, I need to use *my* best weapon." And
he faded into the shadows of the forest around me.

Ceph had a point. I veered into my beetle form and
flew up to a low branch, where I could see the enemy
coming.

And come they did. It seemed like an unstoppable
wave, a line of men so long it faded into the forest on
either side. They wore armor of red and black, one
looking exactly like another; a faceless horde.

Easier to kill that way, Iomu said, slightly more sedate.
You ready for this?

Yeah, I said, not relishing the thought of how many
men I might kill tonight.

They'd kill you first, in a heartbeat.

I know, but that doesn't make it easier.

Iomu sighed and gave the impression of a nod. She
understood, for all her bluster.

And the time had come to act. I jumped off my branch into a group, transformed and spun, hacking them down like wheat. Unlike the last fight, there were few here with ranged weapons ready. So, as they came out of the forest, an unending wave, of men, I cut them down. And around me I heard other sounds of fighting. Men and women, fighting for their lives and the lives of their friends and families.

I had to keep moving, or the pile of bodies around me would have grown too high and hindered me. I hopped — in beetle form — from place to place, wreaking havoc upon the waves of soldiers. Until one of my hops took me into a small clearing.

Here, a group of men were guarding some others who had maps out, and a make-shift table already set up... some form of forward command post.

I buzzed over in beetle form, then transformed amidst the men at the center of the clearing and with three strokes of my sword they were all down. The men guarding the clearing turned inward and rushed me. I fought like a man possessed, and though some few of their attacks reached through my defenses to slide off my armor or cut shallow gashes into me... I cut them down until there were no more. Then, in a rage, I cut up the table that had been set up here.

But then I heard the heavy flapping of wings above me.

My heart turned to ice.

I prayed it would be Lyran, but when I looked up, the

shadow of a dragon above me was far larger than Eophon.

"Spirits," I breathed.

Then something fell from that massive shadow, and a man landed on his feet, with a heavy thud, in the clearing with me. He was huge, as big as I was, his sword even larger than mine.

"Did you do all of this?" he asked in a rumbling deep voice.

"I did."

"Impressive. You may actually be more of a challenge than my pitiful brother was."

Was? What had happened to Lyran?

I steeled myself. I couldn't think about that now. I had a dragon lord to deal with. And if what I'd learned from Lyran was true, he was even stronger than I was. I didn't much want to find out.

"I'll make you a deal," Aaghar said. "If you can get three cuts on me, I'll take my men and go. I've already dealt with my brother. The rest of you are no real threat to me."

What do you think? I asked Iomu.

Ah... It was the first time I'd ever heard her the least bit hesitant. But then she seemed to pull from some store of resolve. *If anyone can do it, you can, Rhino. I believe in you!*

The dragon lord had already dealt with Lyran, or so he'd said, and I'd always considered Lyran to be my superior in combat... could I take this man? The real question was: did I have a choice? If I didn't, he'd continue this onslaught and others would die.

"Deal," I said, and set myself.

Aaghar stalked around me slowly, head tilting, studying me, as well as the scene around me. "Decent form. Obvious strength. Armor is a bit lacking. That sword is well made though." He finally stopped his movement and set himself. "I give you one chance in ten. Come at me."

We both waited for a long moment. "I can wait all night," he said. "And the longer you wait, the more of your friends and allies die."

Spirits, he was right. I moved in slowly, carefully. Then... I stopped.

I'd been about to face him head on, and that was the stupidest thing I could have done.

Remember your hit and fade technique, Ceph's voice came to me.

I smiled.

I charged at the dragon lord, then, just before I would have entered his range, I veered and pulled myself up, above him, changing back to come crashing down on him. He hadn't been expecting that, clearly a bit stunned by my seeming disappearance. I roared as I drove my sword down onto his helm. The metal gave and split, but my sword slid off to one side instead of cleaving into his head. Instead, I hit the heavy armor covering his shoulder. I tore through most of that and I may have nicked him. By the Spirits, he had a lot of armor.

I landed behind him and veered as he spun, this time sinking low as that massive blade of his cleaved the air where I had been.

"Oh, you're a tricky one! I can see how you defeated so many of my men!" he said, but actually sounded... happy. His voice was alive with delight.

I appeared and swung low, my sword biting into his thigh, but he must have been expecting some attack and his blade blocked mine from progressing much deeper... or else I might have cut off his leg entirely.

Still, he leapt back and landed awkwardly, limping.

"That's two cuts," he said with a grin. "One away from victory."

So... I *had* nicked his shoulder.

I rose and studied him for a moment. He was favoring his leg and his helm was off, his long dark hair blew about his face, a possible distraction.

I veered and buzzed up high as he looked around frantically.

Just one more hit.

I flew around behind him and returned to myself, a swing at his unprotected head. He ducked and spun and suddenly my blade was slicing through nothing while his was cleaving toward my side. I veered as his blade passed through where I'd been, then transformed back now that the blade was past me.

But I think that's what he'd intended all along. My focus was on his blade, and I missed his off-hand fist, which caught me in the center of my chest.

I felt like I'd been hit by a charging bull and was thrown back, some distance, crashing through trees to land hard on my back.

I couldn't breathe. I tried desperately to get air, making odd sucking-gasping noises. But there was too much pressure on my chest. I looked down to see my armor caved in far too deeply. He'd punched me so hard my armor was now restricting my breathing, pressing hard into my chest, which also hurt like nothing I'd ever felt before, a stinging ache with each attempted breath.

Then Aaghar was there next to me, laughing. "You almost had me, a worthy foe indeed. But, not worthy enough."

I tried to move, tried to roll away, but he put a hand on my shoulder, stopping me with incredible strength and a vise-like grip. Then his other fist came for my face.

And that is all I remember.

CHAPTER 22

PAN

Everything was going to The Pits, fast.

In the deep of night, sounds of fighting echoed from all around us in the forest. Ceph and Rhino had been part of the line meant to hold back the dragon lord's forces, but it sounded like they'd failed. Swift, Falcon, and I were protecting Dawn and Roo. And the two ladies were at the end of a long line of refugees helping to get them through the forest and away. But with a growing forest fire to one side and an approaching army on the other, I was growing less and less certain we'd escape.

Some of Lyran's original militia had been escorting the refugees, but were now breaking off, moving through the forest to try to keep the approaching army away from their loved ones.

Tensions were high and every snapped twig and hoot of an owl had people jumping.

Keep calm and levelheaded, you are true-born Fey,

stronger than any man and Bonded to me, together we can make it through this and help those we love. Eona was stalwart and sure.

Thank you, I said to her. I'd needed those strengthening words.

And once I was level-headed and trying to think logically about how best to protect Dawn, Roo, and the others, I hit upon a dilemma: to keep Ceph's borrowed spirit-gift or... acquire Dawn's. Without Ceph's gift I wouldn't be able to heal anyone if they were hurt. That was a grave consideration. The trouble was, before people got hurt there would be fighting and without Dawn's gift, I was only a passable warrior.

I knew Fey hand-fighting but had never mastered it. And having travelled and trained with Lyran these past few months, I had learned a lot and could hold my own against any average fighter now, but against an army? With Dawn's gift I could better protect myself and others, and hopefully they wouldn't get seriously hurt.

Any other considerations? I asked Eona?

You have laid out the arguments well. As loath as I would be to lose a healing ability, if you cannot defend yourself, and you are hurt to the point of unconsciousness, it wouldn't matter anyway. Better to fight and hopefully stay alive longer.

Agreed.

"Dawn,' I whispered, next to her in the darkness. She looked to me, and I reached out my hand. She took it. "I'm going to borrow your gift."

She smiled and nodded. "Use it well."

I replaced Ceph's ability with Dawn's spirit-gift of *connectedness*, and instantly felt a strange *knowing*. Simply from observing small cues, I could tell Dawn was on edge and Roo was afraid. The twins were ready for a fight, and were glad they were together after so long, but still uncertain of their abilities in an all-out battle. The brush of the wind and the wave of heat from the fire — slowly approaching on our left — were all taken in by my gift and I knew how close we were to the flames, how long it might be until they overwhelmed us. And those sounds of distant combat told me that forces were approaching... but slowly. Whatever our warriors out there were doing, it was slowing the advance, either that or the darkness and thick forest was aiding us.

We moved out from thick forest into a large cleared area. The moon was out, and I could see that a previous fire had thinned the trees here. The river which had been close to our camp, ran through the middle of this area and our column was following its flow eastward.

Ahead of me, Dawn froze. She looked up and I sensed it too, something flying above the trees, approaching. It wasn't the dragon lord, my senses told me it was small.

And over the moon a large bird glided, shadowed before banking hard and coming to land on the far side of the river.

The bird transformed into a woman.

Swan.

"Pits!" Dawn swore. "Not here, not now!"

Dawn moved in front of Roo, and I moved to get in front of Dawn, as did Swift and Falcon.

"I finally found you, little one." Swan laughed as she said the words. "Now, to get rid of the rest of these pesky insects." She put her hands together, palms facing out and a thick beam of dark red energy erupted from her. But it wasn't meant for us. Screams echoed and died as those at the end of the line of refugees were incinerated. The remaining refugees were running now, scrambling to get away and find safety in the forest.

"No!" Dawn and Roo screamed at once.

"Why?" Dawn pleaded.

"So we can be alone," Swan said with a manic grin in the moonlight. Swan motioned to we three men and Roo. "I don't care about the rest of you. Dawn, do the right thing and come with me. I promise, if you come quietly these others will live." She seemed sincere, but my senses told me she was also completely insane, and I didn't think we could trust anything she said. "And... I'll only torture you a little. A lady must have her fun."

"We won't let you take her!" Falcon said and in the next instant he and Swift had veered, flying across the river to Swan and reverting back. They charged in... but something was wrong. I could feel it. Dawn must have felt it too.

"Watch out!" she cried, but it was too late.

Swan hadn't been worried, hadn't even tried to defend herself against the two attacks. Falcon and Swift's weapons bounced off some invisible field around the woman. Swan then waved her hands out to the sides and the twins went flying in opposite directions as if swatted by some giant, unseen hand. They flew dozens of feet, crashing through low brush and the trunks of dead trees, before landing hard. Neither of them moved.

"That was stupid," Swan said. "I'll give you one more chance to come to me, Dawn, or these other two will also die." She vaguely waved at myself and Roo.

"I can't... influence her emotions. It's like there is something in the way!" Roo hissed.

Swan veered and took a quick flight over the river. She returned to herself, now only a half-dozen feet from us. "What will it be, Dawn?"

"How did you find us?" Dawn asked. I sensed she was buying time, trying to figure out Swan's weaknesses.

Swan grinned. "The little princeling of Basia. He said he'd join our side, if we let his sister go, so Aaghar did just that. The Basian princess is free now... well, free from her life anyway." Swan giggled. "We did have some fun torturing her to death. Aaghar never liked her anyway, a little too shy and quiet. He likes a woman who screams when he's inside her. And with that incredible strength of his, he is quite the lover." So, Swan was in league with the dragon lord. She confirmed that when she said, "I met the wonderful man when I came west to find you. We took an instant liking to each other. And when the Basian prince fell into our lap, and wanted so much to help us, we agreed." She laughed. "And you played right into our hand. We'd always meant to let him go so he could return to this camp and let us know where you were. You're escape with him was incredibly well timed. We let it happen and waited for his signal. And when this is all over and I've killed you in front of your mother, then... killed your mother and her entire family, I'll return to my dragon prince and we'll rule these lands together."

"You want Dawn alive so you can kill her?" Roo said incredulous.

Swan looked a bit affronted. "Why of course. She's not the true prize. It's her mother who I wish to torture. She took everything from me, and I'll take everything from her. And what better way to do that, than to slowly kill her daughter in front of her."

"You're not making much of a case for why I should come with you," Dawn said sourly.

"Your friends will live, that is what you get if you come easily. Also, you'll remain alive for a while longer, until Aaghar and I conquer Elista. But... if you don't—"

I'd heard enough. I attacked, sensing her lack of attention on me... I drove in, my sword slashing at her heart. Yet as fast as I was... Swan moved with speed I didn't expect and even with my gift of senses and knowing, I couldn't track her. She stepped out of the way of my strike and in toward me. I felt it before I saw it... her dagger plunging into my chest. I fell back, landing hard.

I heard Dawn's scream: "No! Pan!"

I was shocked for a moment and couldn't move. I felt wet warmth welling and flowing freely from my chest, while the rest of me began to grow cold. I couldn't think, couldn't react. I just lay there while Swan laughed. She wiped off the dagger, staining her white clothes with crimson; my blood. She didn't seem to care.

I couldn't believe it. One quick strike had been all it had taken to drop me, even with my toughened hide.

No! Pan, get up! There is still strength in you! Eona tried to rouse me. *Bloody Bones, why did we give up the healing gift?*

I had to agree. I hadn't seen this fate coming at all. Yet, for all my efforts to rise, to move, all I succeeded in doing was groan in pain and twitch. My strength had left me. Too much blood was welling up out of my heart.

My heart...

Dawn...

With that thought I managed to move, sit up, I swiped my sword at Swan's leg. But she deftly leaped out of the way and landed on me, one foot on my chest, another on my face. I was thrown back to the ground.

That had been my last attempt. With it, I'd caused even more blood to spill from my chest... and now I was growing far too cold. I couldn't feel my legs and my arms were starting to go numb.

Swan laughed. My ears could still hear well enough. "One more down, will you sacrifice your friend here too, Dawn? Or... Ohh! I have an even better idea. I'll take you both and use your friend to make sure you do as I ask. Yes, that will work wonders."

"You and what army?" Dawn hissed.

"That one!" Swan said, and I heard the heavy footfalls

of many men flooding out from the trees. "Well, that was well timed indeed. Now surrender or... or I won't kill your friend quickly at all, I'll make it nice and slow. Perhaps I'll hand her over to Aaghar. He'd enjoy torturing her. He likes the soft ones, pulling them apart slowly."

And as I faded into darkness and the last of my warmth fled, I heard Swan's laughter and the sounds of fighting. Then... nothing.

To be continued...

Don't miss the next book in the series!

Double Doom
Shadows Over Elista: Book Four

Can they survive the full force of a dragon lord's army?

Roo and Dawn are finally reunited, having assembled a force of armed men and refugees from all corners of the empire. Their trials have changed them, made them stronger and more confident; in themselves and their love. For Roo, her past is behind her and before her lies a brilliant future filled with adoring men and a sister-in-spirit who knows her unlike any other. While for Dawn, the walls around her heart have fallen and she's no longer shying away from the love being offered by all her men.

It seems like nothing can stop these two women and the men who follow them. But, when a combined force of the dragon lord Aaghar, and the dastardly Swan, find the renegade camp, everything is thrown into chaos.

All that Roo and Dawn have worked for teeters on the brink of collapse, and the path ahead is filled with trials that will test the bonds of their sisterhood, the limits of their abilities, and the true depths of their guys' love.

OTHER BOOKS BY CLARA WILS

THE GRECIAN GODDESS TRILOGY

Kiss of the Goddess, book 1

Power of the Goddess, book 2

Bonds of the Goddess, book 3

THE MISTS OF ELISTA TRILOGY

Bonds and Blood, book 1

Shape and Shadows, book 2

Form and Fury, book 3

SHADOWS OVER ELISTA

Double Discover, book 1

Double Danger, book 2

Double Disaster, book 3

Double Doom, book 4

Double Destiny, book 5